Winter
in the
High Sierra

~ a Love Story ~

Also by
ROBERT BRIGHTON

Avenging Angel Detective Agency™ Mysteries

The Unsealing

A Murder in Ashwood

Current of Darkness

OTHER TITLES

The Buffalo Butcher

The Phantom of Forest Lawn

Winter in the High Sierra

in the

High Sierra

~ a Love Story ~

ROBERT BRIGHTON

Winter in the High Sierra: A Love Story

A Novel by Robert Brighton

Ashwood Press, the Ashwood Press colophon, Avenging Angel Detective
Agency, and the Angel colophon are trademarks of Copper Nickel, LLC

Cover and Interior Design by The Book Cover Whisperer

978-1-964015-91-0 Paperback
978-1-964015-90-3 Hardcover
978-1-964015-92-7 eBook
978-1-964015-93-4 Audiobook

Library of Congress Control Number: 2024933544

Find out more at
RobertBrightonAuthor.com

FIRST EDITION

For Paul E. Houser

Teacher, Mentor, Friend

Contents

By Way of Introduction

For those who have read any of my other novels to date, *Winter in the High Sierra* will be quite a departure. While it is set primarily in 1900—in the middle of the time period I especially favor—everything else is different from my previous outings.

The biggest departure is that *Sierra* is fundamentally a *romance*. Frankly, that was not a genre I thought that I'd explore, mainly because I've never written (nor read) a romance novel. But my publisher suggested that I give it a try. I took up the gauntlet, and this is the result. So I suppose you could say that this is my *idea* of a romance novel. Or, perhaps more accurately, a love story.

Writing *Sierra* led to something and somewhere quite unexpected. I quickly found myself warming to my story, and especially to my characters. To such a degree, in fact, that I could hardly wait to dive back into their world each day and follow them as they confronted both the challenges of survival and the even bigger challenges of figuring out something about the larger significance of their lives—and of life itself.

I enjoyed the writing so much that I completed the book in record time, and sent it on its way. But to my great surprise—and after I had recorded the entire audiobook version—something very unfortunate happened, and I found the manuscript back in my hands. At first, I was dismayed and disappointed, since I'd been so eager to see the book in print. Just as I was about to despair of the whole project, I decided—without any better plan in mind—to read the manuscript again.

It was then that the silver lining to my little dark cloud revealed itself.

In rereading the original *Sierra*—which was certainly a *good* book—I discovered hidden inside, waiting to be teased out, the elements of a *much better* book. So with renewed purpose I rewrote the whole thing, not as a chore but as a labor of love. And out of my despair emerged something beautiful and joyous: a better book, a more satisfying book, a book that made me laugh and cry.

In this story about two "lost" people, I hope to have captured something of what most of us have to struggle with and through in our lives—personal growth, grief, regret, the problems of self-definition and self-love, and the nature of redemption.

Whether in the trackless wilderness of the High Sierra, or in the sometimes-bewildering depths of our own hearts and minds, I believe that—while we may wander for quite a while—we are never truly lost, unless and until we give up.

I'm glad I didn't give up on *Winter in the High Sierra*.

A couple of small final notes. I recognize that 'Sierra' is, in fact, a plural noun—though in 1900 'High Sierra,' 'High Sierras,' and 'Sierras' were all used interchangeably to describe these mountains. Thus I have chosen to use 'High Sierra' and 'Sierras' in order to stay closer to period usages.

Last: to understand 1900 dollar values in modern terms, multiply them by forty or fifty.

Robert Brighton

Où sont les neiges d'antan?

— François Villon, *Ballade des dames du temps jadis*, 1461

1

Last Train to Frisco

November 1899
Eight Miles West of Truckee, California

The Sierra Pacific train—six passenger cars and a baggage car behind one big steam locomotive and its coal tender—heaved itself painfully up the steep slopes of the rugged Sierra Nevada mountains, its great wheels slipping on the slick rails. As the train strained skyward, heavy snow began to fall and halfway to the summit turned into a whirling blizzard. Even when leaning perilously out of the side window of his cab, the engineer could no longer tell the difference between earth and sky.

He slowed his engine to a crawl. The slow creep helped avoid the danger of plowing into an unseen snowdrift or fallen tree, but it made it even more difficult to get any traction. The locomotive's supply of sand—shot from a steam hose onto the rails in front of the great driven wheels—had long since been exhausted.

Suddenly, just ahead, something enormous loomed up out of whistling whiteness.

"All stop! *Avalanche*!!" the engineer called out, and the fireman quickly banked his coals. The train slowed still further, and then stopped entirely—trapped in a narrow pass by a slide of snow at least half as high as the locomotive itself. The iron beast sat there hissing in frustration.

"Send out the digging crew," the engineer told his fireman. "The way it's coming down now, if we don't get this cleared away quickly, we'll be stuck for good." The fireman jumped down from the cab and struggled back through the deep snow toward the passenger cars.

After a long minute, six men with coal shovels bailed out of the first passenger car and attacked the mound of snow. The conductor also waded forward and climbed up into the cab with his engineer.

"What should I tell the passengers?" the conductor asked.

The engineer took off his cap and wiped his forehead on his sleeve. "Tell them the truth. That this is the worst storm I've ever seen, and that we're moving heaven and earth to get under way again."

"They're not going to like that much."

"You don't say? I don't like it much, either—but that's what we are facing."

"Understood," the conductor said, and jumped down from the cab.

Two long hours later, the breathless foreman of the digging crew walked back to the locomotive and called up to the engineer through cupped hands.

"I've never seen it this bad," he yelled. "It's coming down faster than we can clear it away."

"You *have* to clear it!" the engineer shouted down. "If we don't get going again, everyone dies!"

The foreman seemed to gather up his nerve. "Not to tell you your business, sir, but even if we *can* get her moving again, there's no way she can pull all this weight"—he gestured down the length of the train— "over the summit. Not with the tracks in this condition."

The last train of the season was always a gamble in the High Sierra, a race against the arrival of the first squalls of winter. The engineer knew that the foreman was right—the cards had fallen against his machine.

He nodded down at the man. "Dig like your life depends on it, then," he said, "until you can't dig anymore." The man trotted back to his crew, and the engineer pulled the bell for the conductor.

"You have news?" the conductor asked when he arrived, his tidy uniform coated up to his chest in snow.

"I do, but it's not *good* news," the engineer replied. "You'll have to get the passengers to move forward into the first two cars. Pack 'em in like sardines, if need be. To have any chance at making it out of these damned hills, I'll have to leave behind three of the passenger cars, the baggage car, that private car at the end, and every spare pound of coal we don't need."

"You must be joking!"

"Do I look like I'm joking?" the engineer snarled. "It's either that or everyone freezes to death right here. These mountains—and this pass—have killed a lot of people, and I'm not about to add to the total."

The conductor nodded and went back to his cars, where he began herding the passengers forward. "Hand luggage only!" he instructed. "We have to leave the baggage car behind. The railroad will deliver your belongings to you in the spring."

This caused an uproar. "It's not what any of us wants to do," he said, holding out his hands. "But there's no other choice. We either get out of these mountains before nightfall, or we'll be stuck here."

"So what?" a man's voice called out. "They'll send another train to pull us out."

"Five *months* from now, they will," the conductor replied. "And we won't last five *days* in this cold. If you want to stay alive, you'll do as I say and *move*, and on the double!"

While the passengers were jostling forward, the conductor jumped down from the train to retrieve the lone passenger in the private car at the rear of the train, just behind the baggage car. It was a so-called palace car, which boasted every possible luxury—fine linens, fine food, and its own iron stove to keep it toasty warm. Unlike the other passenger cars, though, by design it had no through connection to the rest of the train. People who could afford to travel in palace cars could afford their privacy.

The conductor fought the snow all the way back to the palace car, where he found the door either locked or frozen tight. "*Miss!*" he shouted, banging on it with his palm. "Open up! We have an emergency! *Miss!*"

There was no reply—not a sound nor a movement from inside the car. The conductor hammered on the door for two full minutes more, but to no avail.

"Mister conductor!" a muffled voice called out behind him. The conductor turned to see the foreman of the digging crew, bundled up to his eyes against the driving snow.

"The engineer says we're out of time," the man yelled. "We've cleared as much snow as we can. The cars have been uncoupled, and the coal's off-loaded. So we've got to get under way—now!"

"But there's a young woman still in this car!" the conductor yelled back. "We can't leave her here to die!"

"The engineer says we have no other choice!" the foreman said. "It's either her or—"

His voice was drowned out by a deep rumble from the reawakened engine, reverberating over the snow. Ahead of them a column of thick black smoke belched into the sky.

The conductor and the foreman turned and fought their way back to the second passenger car—now the rearmost of the train, and packed with people. As he swung aboard, the conductor looked back over his shoulder, hoping against hope that the young woman would be following. Or waving. Or anything.

She was not.

When the engineer pushed the throttle forward, at first his machine responded by drifting *backward*, in the direction of the severed rear of the train—seemingly as reluctant as its conductor to abandon the young woman to her fate. Desperate, the engineer laid on every bit of the mighty engine's power—and with a surly bellow of protest, the great locomotive began at last to advance. The big steel tires slipped and grabbed, but little by little the amputated train gained its footing.

As what remained of the last train to Frisco laboriously pulled free of its snow trap, the three empty passenger cars, baggage car, and the palace car were left behind in the swirling snow.

In the palace car at the rear of the train, Louisa MacGregor—its sole occupant—had taken a sleeping draught shortly after her luncheon. Her father himself had seen her to the station in New York City, as if concerned she might decide not to go at all. Yet Louisa was duly shut up in her gilded cage, and off the train had gone, bound for San Francisco, where her brother and his family lived.

Her father had thought the change of scenery would help heal his daughter's broken heart. But as the Frisco Express churned westward, all Louisa could do was replay the past few painful months: her wedding plans wrecked by her fiancé's parents, who had from the start objected to the union. From their vantage point atop the pinnacle of

New York's old money elite, Louisa's would-be in-laws saw even the rather distinguished MacGregor family as little more than upstarts and social climbers. Eventually they succeeded in derailing the young couple's planned nuptials.

Louisa's wounds were still fresh when, in a last cruel spasm of fate, her former fiancé—bereft over the loss of his intended—vanished from the afterdeck of the Long Island Ferry. Officially, the event had been ruled an accident, a terrible mishap—but Louisa and everyone else knew that it had been suicide.

No luxurious trip across country could offer sanctuary from such bitter memories. And so she had begun quaffing her sleeping potion at almost any hour of the day, seeking oblivion in a drug called laudanum—a powerful mix of opium and alcohol. Before being hustled aboard her train, Louisa had taken stealthy care to obtain a fresh bottle from a cooperative druggist on the Lower East Side.

Thus when the Frisco Express stalled in the deep and deadly snows of the High Sierra, Louisa MacGregor was warmly cocooned in her sleeping quarters, lost in an opium dream. She didn't feel the train lurch to a halt, didn't hear the conductor's shouted entreaties, and didn't sense the stillness of her forsaken palace car.

Until, that is, she was awakened by a deep, numbing cold. Louisa sat up in bed, threw off her eiderdown duvet, and watched transfixed as her breath turned to steam in the normally cozy car.

What the devil? she thought, getting up and throwing a quilted robe over her dress. Groggily she padded into the parlor, to find that the coal stove had guttered out and an opaque coating of ice had formed on the windows of the palace car. Outside there was nothing but white.

It was obvious that the train had stopped, so she rang the bell for the conductor to learn what was amiss. When after a few minutes the conductor didn't show up, she screwed up her courage, pulled open the palace car door, and gingerly stepped onto the corrugated iron stairs—or tried to. All but the topmost tread were covered in freshly fallen snow. She turned away from the wind and looked toward the rear of the stopped train.

Since Louisa's car was the last one, behind her was nothing, only snow-covered tracks disappearing into the blowing snow. This gave her no particular surprise or alarm—until she turned and squinted upwind. It was difficult to make anything out while being pelted with huge, high-velocity snowflakes, but when she angled her hand just so to shield her eyes, she finally grasped the immensity of her problem. The locomotive was *gone*, and with it half of the train. Left behind on the tracks, with snowdrifts piling up against them, were three empty passenger cars, the baggage car, and her palace car.

Stunned, Louisa hurried back inside—the car was cold, but at least she was out of the wind—and sat down weakly on the velvet couch in the parlor. She almost began to weep, and then reminded herself that tears were useless. She had to *do* something. But what?

Wait for the next train? That wasn't a possibility. She knew very well that hers had been the last of the year, and that her father had taken pains to persuade the Sierra Pacific to allow her car to come along with it. *Hope for a rescue mission?* Without a doubt, her father would mount one—but by the time word got to him in New York that her car had been abandoned, she would be long dead of starvation or cold.

That left only one thing: a hike out of the mountains, however improbable it seemed to cross the spine of the Sierras on foot and in the teeth of winter. *At least I would die trying*, Louisa thought. She drew her robe closer around her and was envisioning the probable end of her life, when outside one of her snow-smeared windows she spied a large, dark shape shambling down the hill toward the tracks. It resembled one of the grizzly bears she had heard and read about. *So much for walking.*

She studied the creature as it lumbered down the snowy slope, and as it came closer she could make out that it was no bear at all, but a man shuffling along on snowshoes, wearing an enormous buffalo robe over his shoulders and a battered hat tied to his head with a woolen scarf. He was accompanied by a large and ferocious-looking dog. Louisa had learned the hard way that humans are at least as deadly as bears—and considerably less direct—so she shrank down below the windowsill, peeping out every few seconds to follow the bear-man's path.

He reached the side of her car, looked one way and the other, and then trudged toward the first car of what remained of the train. She lost him to view for quite some time, until his shadow suddenly blocked the early light sneaking through her icy window. Louisa shrank down again, just as the bear-man began thumping on the door.

She assumed he'd give up in time and go back to wherever he'd come from, and after a few seconds the pounding did indeed stop. But then she heard a quieter sound—that of the man tinkering with the lock. *A bandit!* she thought. *He thinks that there must be valuables in here!* Crouching low, she slunk into her sleeping compartment and wriggled under the bed, though first grabbing the tiny derringer that was sitting on her nightstand. Her father had given it to her at the station, without any explanation whatsoever—as though she could divine how in the world to use a firearm.

Louisa had pulled the edge of the bedspread down to conceal herself when she felt a sudden blast of winter whip along the floor of the car as the carriage door opened. Then it slammed again.

"Is anyone here?" a voice said.

She tried to hold her breath and listen as the man began nosing around in her parlor. She heard the sound of loud, appreciative chewing—he must have found the remains of her luncheon sandwich. She heard his voice say, "Try this, mutt—it's delicious!"

Why, he's eating my luncheon! And giving it to his horrid dog, at that, she thought.

The bear-man's footsteps approached her sleeping quarters, and from the entryway his deep voice was as clear as if he were under the bed with her. "Is anyone in here?" he repeated. She could see his snowy boots dripping meltwater onto the Oriental rug.

Huddled on the freezing floor of the palace car, Louisa had never been so cold—and just as the man's feet turned to go, to her horror her teeth began chattering like castanets. The feet slowly turned back around. "*Who's in here?*" he said, more softly, and the feet approached the bed. She held her breath again until she thought her lungs would burst, but damned if the telltale chattering didn't begin again. She gripped the derringer as the feet came to rest beside her hiding spot.

The bedspread slowly rose, and the man knelt to peer under it. At first, all Louisa could see was a big beard caked with gobbets of snow, and a pair of very blue eyes. She thrust out her little gun.

"L-l-leave m-m-me alone!" she said. "I m-mean it. I'll p-p-pull the tr-tr-trigger, I swear!"

The man's face creased into what might have been a tiny smile, making little ripples around the sides of his eyes. "You could, Miss, but it wouldn't do you any good." With that, he reached under the bed and gently removed the derringer from her hand.

"Now come on out of there, and let's talk like regular folk," he said, still looking at her under the bed. "I won't hurt you."

"You'd b-b-better not," Louisa chattered as she crawled out of concealment and stood.

The man's dog—a big, brindled thing with an enormous, flat skull—cocked his head and looked at her quizzically. The bear-man himself was tall, at least six feet, and under his giant buffalo robe he seemed to take up twice as much space as any normal man. His big beard and thick, wavy brown hair framed a rugged, handsome face punctuated by those two piercing blue eyes.

"Hello," he said in a soft baritone, taking a half step toward her.

"You stay b-b-back!" she said, summoning all of her martial spirit. "I'll have you know that I'd sooner die, right here and now, than be *r-r-ravished* by the likes of you!"

There was that little could-be smile again, which the dog seemed to share.

"I didn't come here to ravish anyone," the bear-man said. "I saw the smoke from the locomotive stop for quite a while, and then start up again. I figured they were stuck, so I came down the mountain to see if I could help out."

"Unfortunately," Louisa said, drawing her robe still more tightly around herself, "you're a little late. As you can see, the train has gone and left me behind."

"I noticed that," he said dryly.

"You have quite the nerve, sir, to make sport of my predicament!" she said, flustered. "Now, if you please, leave me in peace and go back to wherever you came from." She waved at him with the back of her hand.

"Well, that might not be possible."

"And whyever not?"

"I'm from New York."

She stamped her foot. "I did not mean *literally* for you to return to whatever place from which you might have originated," she said. "I meant, go back up that hill to wherever your . . . lair is!"

"My *lair*," he said thoughtfully. "For the record, Miss, that's not a *hill*. That's a *mountain*. But in any case, you can't stay here. You'll have to come with me. To my lair."

"Over my dead body!"

"That's exactly what I'm trying to avoid. Look how cold you are already. You've got no heat, and whatever coal the train left behind is already two feet deep in snow. If you think it's cold now, you cannot imagine how much colder it will get as soon as that sun goes down behind the trees. I have a cabin—or *lair* if you prefer—about an hour's hike from here. If you want to live, you'll come with me and stay there."

"And if I refuse?" Louisa demanded.

"I haven't thought that far ahead," Bear-Man said. "We've only just met."

"Oooh, you! You are *impossible*! I *knew* I ought to have shot you when I had the chance."

"You wouldn't have shot me."

"You don't think so? In case you didn't notice, I had my finger on the trigger and was ready to fire!"

"But you hadn't pulled back the hammer and cocked the thing," he said. "You could have tried to fire it for all you were worth, and I'd still be standing here unharmed."

"You are a terrible, awful man!"

"Look, Miss, maybe I am, and maybe I'm not. But if we don't get going pretty soon, we're going to be stranded for good. Here, you'll need this." He slipped the giant buffalo robe from his shoulders and draped it over hers, almost collapsing Louisa under its weight. From a small pack he had kept under his robe, he removed a pair of big, furry mittens.

"Hold out your hands," he said. She did, and he stuck them on one by one. He finished her ensemble by removing his hat and plopping it down over her eyes.

"You look very fashionable," he said. "Oh, and before we go, may I ask whom I have the pleasure of rescuing today?"

"You are quite a smart aleck," she said. "But if you must know, I am Miss Louisa MacGregor. Also of New York, as it happens."

"Miss MacGregor," he said with a courtly little bow. "A pleasure to meet you, if under difficult circumstances." He turned before she could ask his name in return.

"Now wait here until I come back for you," he said. "And don't lock me out, or you won't make it through the night."

"If only," she muttered, and watched him and his dog go.

Outside, the bear-man shook the snow from two aspen saplings, cut them down with a hatchet he removed from his pack, and then lashed one end of each sapling loosely together with cord. Between this V-shaped frame he strung straps of leather from his pack to fashion a kind of pointed ladder. He attached this contraption to his dog with what looked like a horse's harness, though much smaller. When he had finished, he shuffled back to the palace car.

"Your carriage awaits, Miss MacGregor," he said, trying on what she had grudgingly to admit was a very charming smile. "Shall we?"

Louisa grabbed up her carpetbag from the luggage rack and followed him into the blinding snow, where she found the big dog waiting patiently in his traces, his flat head already an inch deep in fresh flakes. "What's that?" she yelled over the wind, pointing toward the wooden frame.

"It's a dog," he said.

"Not the dog, smarty pants! The other . . . *thing*!"

"Oh! It's called a travois," he shouted back, pronouncing it trah-*vwah*. "We use them up here to haul heavy loads over the snow. Speaking of which . . . just how much do you weigh?"

"I do beg your pardon, sir!" she said indignantly. "*Heavy loads*? And moreover, my *weight* is no concern of yours."

"Look, Miss, while you're busy relaxing on this travois, my mutt and I will be lugging you all the way up that . . . *hill*. He's strong, but even he can pull only about seventy-five pounds, and that's on level ground. Together, he and I can manage a hundred and a quarter— on a good day. So you'll forgive me if I'm a little *concerned* about your *weight*." He squinted at her. "Because I'd say that—while it's diffi-cult to tell under all that—I'd say you go a good buck-ten. Maybe a buck-twenty."

"I refuse to engage in this discussion."

"As you wish. I was merely being polite by asking. In these moun-tains one learns to estimate." Bear-Man cocked his head and examined her. "So . . . I can see you have brown eyes, dark hair, and are approx-imately five feet, five inches tall. And since your velvet dress fits you closely, I won't be far off if I estimate that you run . . . one-fifteen. Give or take."

"My dress, fit notwithstanding, does not allow you to examine and assess my physique."

He shrugged a pair of broad shoulders. "Have it your way. In any case"—he looked up the mountainside—"with you on board, this is going to be a *long* haul."

"You really don't know when to stop, do you?"

She received in reply another rather charming smile. "Now then, Miss MacGregor, I will ask you to lie down on the travois and hang on tight," he said. "Put your bag on your stomach and hold on to it with your free arm. Now snuggle up under that big buffalo robe, and enjoy the ride."

She grumbled, but did as she was told, and watched as he buckled a pair of long straps to the dog's harness and then to a broader band, which he secured across his chest. Leaning forward against his chest strap, he called out, "*Mush, mutt*!" and they were off.

It was a surprisingly smooth ride on the springy travois, and it was much warmer under the buffalo robe than it had been in the palace car. It was clear, however, that Bear-Man and his dog were straining every muscle with each painful, gasping step in the cold, thin air. She wondered if they might not make it to wherever they were going. Bear-Man had given up his hat and robe and mittens for her, and now was facing both a steep climb and a frigid wind whipping down the mountainside. Both must be sapping even his obvious strength, she thought.

After a solid hour of hellish labor, though, they crested a ridge and then—to the great relief of dog, man, and passenger—began a long, snaking descent through a thick stand of lodgepole and ponderosa pines and down into a deep and narrow mountain valley. Everywhere around them was snow, snow, and more snow—except in the distance, where the peaks of the High Sierra bared their teeth. Above the mantle of white draped around their broad shoulders, the jagged mountaintops—vast, muscular masses of cold, bare rock, eternal and unforgiving—shook their fists defiantly at the sky, as though unwilling to concede its crown.

Just as this all-powerful, terrifying landscape seemed ready to swallow her up entirely, Louisa smelled the soft and comforting scent of woodsmoke. Craning her head around the panting dog, she saw ahead a small, tidy cabin with a little half-frozen brook trickling by in front, and with a thin trail of vapor rising gently from its chimney.

They drew up alongside the cabin, and Bear-Man dropped the band from his chest with an exhausted sigh. He unharnessed his dog, helped Louisa up from the travois, and the three of them went inside.

2

Snowbound

*I*nside, the cabin was as tidy as it appeared on the outside—and surprisingly warm—but the air was so foul with what smelled like sewage that Louisa unconsciously pinched her nose shut.

"Sorry about that," Bear-Man said, looking sheepish. "I guess I forgot something this morning." He strode quickly over to a bed in one corner of the cabin and pulled a chamber pot from underneath. He took the offending item outside, was gone for a minute or two, and then returned with the pot, sparkling clean.

"Once I get the fire stoked up again, the air will clear," he said, waving the cabin door open and closed, letting in sharp pulses of cold. "I really am *terribly* sorry about that, but as you may imagine, I wasn't expecting guests."

"It's quite all right," she gasped.

"I promise to be more careful in the future. But who knows—you might well stink up the place yourself sometime." He chuckled.

"Sir, must I remind you that you are addressing a lady?"

"You don't say?" he said with a snicker.

Bear-Man opened the iron door of the woodstove and threw in a few lengths of wood. The flames responded instantly, leaping up behind the mica panels.

"Here, sit down by the fire," he said, pulling up a sturdy chair for her. "I'll make you some coffee, and you'll be warm again in no time."

He busied himself making the coffee while Louisa huddled in front of the stove. From out of nowhere a large, grey cat with copper eyes appeared and curled up quietly at her feet.

"You have a cat, too," she said. "She's beautiful."

"That's Deborah. She keeps the place clear of mice—and does a fine job of it, too. She's so good at it, I almost pity the little things."

Louisa made a face. "I wouldn't spare any sentiment for *mice*."

"Ordinarily I wouldn't mind them, but up here food stores are precious, and mice will spoil them quickly. You may be interested to know the humble housecat was once the most valuable animal in the old mining camps. In the gold rush days, a good mouser could easily command five hundred dollars, which was more than a decent mule. In fact, there were men on Wall Street who made considerable fortunes shipping trainloads of cats out to the goldfields. I suspect that Deborah here is one of their great-great-grandchildren."

"I didn't know that," she said, reaching down to rub the cat's soft belly. "Where did you find her?"

"She found me. Like you did."

Bear-Man's dog sauntered over to examine their new guest, his toe-nails clicking quietly on the board floor. Louisa was afraid of the big brute but forced herself not to pull her hand away when he stuck out his snout to give it a sniff. Someone had told her as a little girl that dogs can sense fear.

"Now will you look at that!" her rescuer said over his shoulder. "Mutt *likes* you. Which is saying something, because he sure doesn't like most people."

"I'm relieved to hear it." She smiled uneasily at the big dog, who smiled back, his tongue lolling pinkly out of one side of his massive jaws. "What's his name, if I may?"

Bear-Man looked at her, somewhat perplexed. "Like I said. Mutt."

"His name is *Mutt*?"

"What's wrong with Mutt? He likes it, and it suits him."

She tentatively patted the dog's flat head, and he squinted in delight.

"Hello Mutt," she said. "My name is Louisa. Good Mutt. Nice doggy." The animal looked steadily back at her, gleefully wagging his tail, and then his whole backside, at the sound of his name in her mouth. He snuffled her hand again and lay on his side beside her chair.

"You've made a friend for life now," Bear-Man said, pouring out two mugs of steaming coffee and handing one to her. "Here you go. I'll fix us something to eat in a little while, after you have a chance to settle in." He took his mug and lay down on the floor, pillowing his head on Mutt's side and stretching his long legs toward the stove.

Louisa blew on the black liquid to cool it, and ventured a sip, expecting it to taste ghastly. To her surprise, it was delicious.

"I am compelled to say," she said, "this is almost as good as the coffee at Delmonico's."

"It ought to be. It *is* Delmonico's."

She didn't know how to reply to that, so they sipped in silence. Louisa glanced around the cabin, and other than the once-neglected chamber pot, everything else in the place was neat as a pin. In the corner of the room, nearest the stove, the bed was made up tidily with a Hudson Bay blanket and a crazy-quilt counterpane on top. Spotless dishware was carefully arrayed in a plate rack mounted to one wall. In addition to her chair, there was a little table, but of good quality, not something that she'd imagined a settler, prospector, or—most likely—a bandit would care to purchase. A broom stood upright near the door, over which hung a hunting rifle.

"You do keep a very tidy home," she said, unable to conceal her amazement.

"It's not like back East, but it is the best one can do in the wilderness."

"How long have you lived up here, if I may ask?"

He took another sip of his coffee. "A little more than three years now. I lose track of time sometimes, though. And I hope I'm not struggling with my English. I don't think I've spoken to anyone in English in almost the whole time. Other than Mutt, of course."

"You are perfectly comprehensible, sir," Louisa said. "In fact, I would say that your vocabulary and articulation are surprisingly like those of an educated man."

He appeared pleased by this and placed his hand over his chest. "Why, thank you, Miss," he said, looking up at her from the floor. "That's kind of you to say."

"I fear I may have been somewhat rude," she said abruptly. "I have neglected to thank you for rescuing me from my predicament. I am in your debt, sir."

"No thanks are necessary, and there's certainly no debt. It's the code out here, where the assistance of a stranger can mean the difference between life and death. If someone needs help, one is obligated to provide it, until that person can again fend for himself. Or, in your case, herself."

"I see," she said, slightly let down by his comment.

They drank their coffee quietly. Mutt squirmed out from under his master and laid his big head on Louisa's tiny shoe.

"What did I tell you?" Bear-Man said. "Mutt thinks there's

something special about you. He just let the back of my cranium hit the floor to be near you."

She leaned over and again patted Mutt on the head, which set his tail a-wagging again, whacking like a bullwhip against the chair leg.

"Sir, I trust that you won't take any offense if I inquire—as much as I do appreciate your rustic hospitality—when might I again be on my way? I was bound for San Francisco to visit my brother and his family, and they'll be worrying about me."

The mountain man lifted his head off the floor and looked at her with that ghost of a smile. "The way this winter's starting off, I'd say . . . April."

"*April*?"

"Yes, April. I'm quite sure yours was to be the last train of the season, and—if you ask me—they were mad even to attempt it this late. The next one won't come through until well after the thaw, when they can clear the tracks and move what's left of yours out of the way. In the meantime, you'll have to stay here with me."

"That's simply absurd," she said, shocked. "I can't very well stay in a little cabin like this—however much nicer it is than one might expect—for an entire winter. With a strange man."

He smiled again, broad and warm this time. "You'll find I'm not all that strange, Miss MacGregor. I tend to be pretty average in most respects. And as I told you on the train, I haven't any desire to hurt you. Believe me, I'd much prefer my solitude, but here we are. We have been thrust together without our consent. By Fate, as it were."

"I don't know how to take that remark."

"Take it as a simple statement of fact. As soon as it's safe for you to leave, I'll make sure we get you back to the tracks and on whatever train is going west. You have my word on it."

"May I at least send a telegraph to my father to let him know that I'm alive?"

"I'm afraid that won't be possible either," he said. "It's miles of wilderness to reach the nearest telegraph station."

"Oh, for heaven's sake! Whatever will we do with ourselves until *April*?"

"We'll be spending a great deal of time in the cabin, of course. Most days, weather permitting, I go out to hunt and forage. There are always chores to do, and I have plenty of books to read."

"*Hunting*?" she said. "*Chores*? Is that all there is to do until spring?"

He looked reassuringly at her. "I didn't mention it, but I'm sure we'll find many compelling topics of conversation. Why, look at how well we're getting along already—just like a couple of old friends."

"We are not *old friends*, sir," she sniffed. "Ours is an acquaintance of happenstance."

"'An acquaintance of happenstance!'" he repeated, bursting into laughter. "What a delightfully rotten term for my . . . rustic hospitality!"

She frowned. "Would you have preferred 'captivity'? That's what first came to my mind."

"It's not all *that* bad, is it? You like my coffee, don't you? Do you think I'd serve up such fine goods to any old captive?"

"We shall see in time," Louisa said. "Perhaps for the present, you might at least tell me your name."

"My name?"

"Yes, your *name*. I know your dog's name. I know your cat's name. So don't you think I ought to know yours?"

He thought for a minute. "Yes, I suppose that does seem reasonable. My name is . . . Littlejohn. Robin Littlejohn, at your service."

Louisa's lip curled in a sarcastic sneer. "*Robin Littlejohn*? Please.

You must take me for a complete idiot. Everyone knows that Robin Hood's best friend was Little John."

He appeared hurt. "Now that's not very nice. I didn't poke fun at 'Louisa MacGregor.'"

"'Louisa MacGregor' isn't a silly made-up name."

"So you say. But you could be Mary Quite Contrary, for all I'd know."

She looked away. "If I could but send a simple telegram from this howling wilderness, my parents would happily confirm my name for your benefit. Be that as it may, I positively *refuse* to call you Mr. Littlejohn. It would only be encouraging you."

"How about Robin?"

"Certainly not Robin. You are emphatically *not* a Robin." She paused and considered. "No, I think instead I'm going to call you Bandit, because that's exactly what I think you are."

He pursed his lips, making his beard dance a little. "All right," he said. "That fits me well enough. Bandit it shall be." He stuck out a strong hand. "Miss MacGregor."

She shook it with some hesitation. "For ease of expression, you may call me Louisa. Since we seem to be trapped here together all winter, a few of the customary niceties are probably best set aside."

He put his stocking feet closer to the hot woodstove and wiggled his toes. "No, I don't think I can call you that."

"Whyever not? It's my *name*."

"While 'Bandit' is an excellent name for a mountain man, 'Louisa' is *far* too prim to suit a mountain lady," he replied. "And that's what you'll have to be, for the next four or five months."

She folded her arms across her chest. "Then what *do* you propose to call me, sir, if not by my given name?"

"I think . . . I think I'll call you *Lou*. Yes, I like Lou."

"'Lou' is a man's name."

"I get the sense that you have more than a little bit of man in you. I might even say that you've got *sand*, Lou. And it's that sand of yours that will keep you alive this winter."

"Sand?"

"Yes, sand. Grit. Toughness. You'll need all of it you can muster over the next few months."

"Oh, after being abandoned in a blizzard, I think I've seen the worst of it."

"Now, Lou, while you are very pretty, and obviously equally intelligent, and I find myself wanting to agree with you . . . in this matter, I regret to inform you that you are wrong. Do not underestimate winter here. What lies ahead has to be seen to be believed."

3

Philosophy

After their introductions were complete, Bandit didn't bother her at all for the rest of the day, but instead allowed Louisa to lose herself in her own thoughts. Occasionally, he'd ask if she wanted something to eat or drink, but her answer was always the same: *I'm not hungry; I'm not thirsty.* At last he convinced her to drink a glass of water, which to her surprise tasted fresher and purer than the water on the train or even back home in Manhattan. But other than that, he let her be.

Mostly she yearned to be back in her palace car—trundling comfortably westward through the beauty of the Sierra Nevada mountains. And even more than indulging in a cozy, scenic ride, she wanted to retrieve the bottle of laudanum from her carpetbag and take a swallow. Only the forgetting potion had the power to chase away all this nightmare and allow her to disappear inside herself, or wherever it was that the opium took her.

The habit had started innocently enough, as a prescription for pain following an emergency operation. Yet she had continued to take it—ten or twenty drops only—continuously after that, because it seemed easier than stopping. But then there had been the breaking off of the engagement, the horrible little cards sent to the would-be guests, the humiliating notice of the rupture published in the society pages of the *New York Times*. She'd thought *that* would be the worst of it, but she hadn't counted on the continuing, daily drip of *scorn*—the feeling that eyes were always upon her, simply because while she had been good enough to be a fiancée, apparently she hadn't been quite good enough to become a wife. And then—in what seemed the very deepest abyss of her despair—there had been the suicide. The word alone—*suicide*—was itself a nearly unendurable burden, and one which seemed could grow no greater; until, that is, the blame for it rolled downhill from the apex of high society and landed squarely atop the already bereft Louisa.

And so she had taken progressively more of the laudanum in an attempt to hold at bay the many evils that beset her. In the nooks and crannies of civilization, it was easy to be discreet about her drug use; she could take it privately in her bedroom or, later on, in her palace car. But now things had been upended, and there was nowhere for her to hide; all of the vastness of the Sierras had been confined within a tiny, secluded cabin.

In such an intimate space, she could not very well begin openly quaffing narcotics, as much as she might like to; that could earn her a one-way trip out into the snow. Worse, as addicts were generally seen to be moral cripples, a great many men would feel it well within their right to take advantage of *that* sort of woman—a defective, desperate one—who would likely be more than willing to do most *anything* just to get her next fix.

As Louisa pondered over her dilemma, Bandit seemed to be in constant motion: cleaning, putting things away, mending a shirt or darning a sock, sharpening a knife. When at last he either tired of chores, or had completed them all, he took down a book from one of several niches he'd cut into the giant logs of the cabin walls. Oddly, Louisa thought, there were at least as many books in this little mountain cabin as there were in her parents' spacious town house on Fifth Avenue.

She was pretending to ignore him when Bandit's voice startled her out of her abstraction.

"Would you like me to read aloud to you?" he asked, holding up his book.

"No, thank you."

"Perhaps you'd like to engage in conversation?"

"About what?"

"Since you've been through so much today, I thought you might benefit from talking about it."

Louisa sniffed. "What good would that do?"

"I don't know. Maybe no good at all." He lit a candle, opened his book, and began to read.

At last curiosity got the better of her. "What *are* you reading, if I may inquire?"

He held up the book. "Nietzsche. Friedrich Nietzsche."

"Who's that?"

"He's a German philosopher, currently very much in vogue in intellectual circles."

"Imagine," she said. "A mountain man in intellectual circles."

"It *is* hard to imagine," he said, without seeming to take the slightest offense. "As for me, though, I don't see what all the fuss is about. I find his philosophy a little discouraging, in fact."

"All philosophy is discouraging, if you ask me."

He set the book down. "That's interesting. Do you ever wonder if it might not be even more discouraging not to have one at all?"

"I can't say that I have, no," she replied, again lapsing into abstraction and wishing she were anywhere else but stranded in the middle of nowhere with the wind howling a gale outside. By now she'd probably be nearing San Francisco, looking forward to a few glasses of good claret and her lovely, decadent sleeping draught.

"I'm very sorry you're stuck here, Lou," Bandit said, reading her mind.

"It's *Louisa*, if you please. Or Miss MacGregor, if you'd don't."

He ignored her. "How about I scratch up some supper for us? Are you hungry yet?"

"Not in the slightest."

"You still have to eat, even if you don't feel like it."

"I most certainly do *not*," she said, crossing her arms.

"Have it your way. But I predict you'll be ravenous by morning. The cold does that."

———— ∿ ————

EVEN THOUGH IT SMELLED quite tasty, she persisted in refusing his supper—some kind of stew. Bandit wasn't deterred by that, ate heartily, and cleaned out his bowl in the snow outside.

"Whew, it's really coming down now," he said when he came back in. "I could barely see my hand in front of my face."

"Oh joy," she said.

They sat close by the hot stove, tired after a long and trying day. Bandit dozed off first, propped up against the side of the bed. Louisa couldn't help herself after that, and a few minutes later lolled off in her chair. As the fire dwindled, the cabin soon became surprisingly cold—not so cold as the palace car, but cold enough. She prodded Bandit awake with her foot.

"I think I'd like to retire for the evening," she said.

"A fine idea. On that score, I have some good news for you—I changed the bedclothes just this morning," he said, gesturing with his head. "So make yourself right at home. I've got to take Mutt out, and then I'll join you."

"You'll *what*? You'll *join* me?"

He gave her a sarcastic look. "Let's see now. There are *two* of us, but only *one* bed."

"There's plenty of room on the floor."

"You don't think I'm going to sleep on a cold *floor* for five months, do you?"

"Well, you certainly won't be sleeping with *me*. And if you refuse to be a gentleman about it, then I suppose I'll have to sleep on the floor."

"You may if you like, but you're going to find it a lot less comfortable than my nice, soft bed. This doesn't have to be such a terrible thing, you know. Just pretend you're sleeping with your sister."

"I don't have a sister, and all the pretending in the world won't change what you are."

"Which is what? Strange?"

"No. A *man*."

He shook his head. "Now that I can't deny. But Lou, believe me, I have no designs on anything other than getting a good night's sleep. It's a lot of work hauling a hundred-twenty-pound lady up a mountainside, you know."

She scowled. "I do not weigh one hundred twenty pounds."

"One-fifteen, minimum."

"*Stop*. Now go and take Mutt outside while I put on my sleeping garment. Since it seems I haven't any choice in the matter, I'll get close to the wall and face away from you."

When Bandit and Mutt returned in a big blast of cold air, Lou was indeed already under the blankets and with her nose pressed against the fragrant pine logs of the cabin wall, which smelled vaguely of butterscotch. Bandit slipped off his jacket, slid his braces over his shoulders, and stepped out of his trousers. He stood beside the bed in his long johns, watching Lou pretend to be asleep.

"I'm getting in now," he said.

"Fine," she said to the wall. "Just make sure you stay on your side of the bed."

"Thank you for reminding me." He doused the candle, slipped under the covers and, as much as she didn't care to admit it, Louisa found it immediately much cozier in the cold cabin with another warm-blooded human beside her. Mutt jumped up on the bed and sprawled across their feet. Deborah joined them a few minutes after, grooming herself noisily after having presumably dispatched another hapless mouse.

"Sleep tight, Lou," Bandit said. "I'm sorry about what's happened to you."

"My name's not Lou, and it's not your fault."

"I know it's not *actually* my fault, but I *am* sorry you're stuck here with me, when you could be having a nice dinner with your brother and his family in San Francisco."

Can this man read minds? she thought.

"Well, I suppose it wasn't meant to be," she said with a sigh. "As my mother would say, we must make the most of whatever trial God sends us."

"You think God brought you here?"

"Who else?"

"Mutt and I did," he said into the darkness.

"I don't mean *literally*. I mean God must have a reason for me to be here."

"You're probably right," Bandit said. "Oh. In the night, if you have to use the thunder mug, wake me up and I'll get out of your way."

"The thunder mug?"

He chuckled in the darkness. "The chamber pot."

"What a crude term. In any case, I made use of it while you were outside."

He made a sniffing sound. "I suspected as much."

"You are a terribly rude man, do you know that?"

"And you are an awfully persnickety woman."

"Take it back."

"I will not. Now get some sleep."

"I'm sure I won't sleep a wink with a big lump like you taking up most of the bed."

His voice softened. "I'll try not to take up too much space. And however inconvenient this whole episode may be, it's better to be here with me than all alone in that palace car. I don't like to think about what you'd be going through right now."

She shivered despite herself. "I *am* grateful for that," she said quietly. "I don't mind saying I thought I was going to die."

"You're safe now," he said. "Now sleep. If we talk about everything tonight, we'll be bored for five months."

"I can scarcely conceive of such a thing."

"And on that tender note, I bid you a peaceful slumber, Lou. If you need anything in the night—or you just feel frightened—wake me up. Whatever you might be feeling, I've felt it already."

I rather doubt that, she thought to herself, and closed her tired eyes. Even without her laudanum, it took only seconds for her to drift away to another place.

4

The Yellow Press

The newspapers had to get wind of it eventually, and when they did they had a field day.

ABANDONED!!

———

Judge's Daughter Left Behind in the Deadly Sierras.

———

RESCUE OUT OF THE QUESTION, EXPERTS SAY.

From Our Wire Service. It is now confirmed that Miss Louisa M. MacGregor, sole daughter of well-known judge James J. MacGregor, of this city, has been lost in the Sierra Nevada mountains of eastern California. After being halted by a severe blizzard, the Sierra Pacific Railroad's engineer inexplicably uncoupled the young woman's car before continuing on to San Francisco. Thus the unfortunate Miss MacGregor was left stranded in one of the most remote reaches of the forbidding mountain range.

This newspaper has consulted with a number of noted

*authorities associated with the New York Explorers'
Club, and all agree that there can be no possibility of
relief or rescue until spring when the deep snows, for
which the area is notorious, finally release their grip on
the mountains.*

*This is the second time in only months that misfortune
has visited the MacGregor family. It will be remembered that recently Miss MacGregor was the subject of
considerable talk among New York society, after having
been jilted by a young man of high rank. The erstwhile
claimant to the hand of lovely Miss MacGregor died
soon after in mysterious circumstances. It is believed
that Miss MacGregor was going to the West to forget her
recent troubles.*

In disgust, Judge MacGregor threw the newspaper down on his
breakfast table. "Damned yellow press!" he snarled, smacking his hand
on the table and making the crockery dance. "They're positively gleeful
about this. And *jilted*? It's adding insult to injury!"

"James," his wife said, dabbing her eyes with her napkin, "you
know very well that no good can come of getting worked up over the
newspaper. We must not allow them to add to our troubles. We will
have more than enough as it is. But we will face them together, as we
have so many others."

He leaned back and looked at the ornate plaster ceiling of their
town house. "You cannot know what I would give to possess a fraction
of your tranquility," he said. "If it were not for you, Julia, I would come
entirely unmoored."

"A terrible thing has happened, and we cannot pretend that it has not," she said. "All we can do is to endure it, as best we know how."

"You are a remarkable woman, my dear. I see where our Louisa got her strength."

"And from you she learned sound judgment. She is a resourceful girl, and she may find a way out of this predicament."

Judge MacGregor looked away, blinking. "I wish I could believe that, but it seems that it would require a miracle."

Mrs. MacGregor got up, came around the table, and knelt next to her husband. "God blessed us with a wonderful daughter, husband. Perhaps he will also bless us with a miracle."

"I will try to believe that."

She looked up at him. "We must not let our faith waver when we need it most. Let us both imagine that God will send an angel to watch over our dear Louisa."

The judge turned and embraced his wife, hiding his tears in her hair. "Yes, a guardian angel," he whispered. "Lord, send your angel to watch over our lost daughter. Restore her to us, if it be thy will."

"Amen," Mrs. MacGregor said.

5

✦

What I've Missed

When she peeked out from under the blankets on her first morning in the cabin, there was no sign of Bandit or of Mutt. This gave Louisa some time to examine her temporary refuge in greater detail.

The cabin was a stout log oblong, probably twenty feet long by fifteen wide, with two small glass windows set deep in each long wall. At one end of the cabin was the woodstove, flanked by the bed on one side and the table and chair on the other. There was nothing in the middle of the board floor except a large and rather fine Oriental rug, which struck Louisa as an incongruity in a rustic mountain cabin. On the far end of the structure were a tall cupboard, a huge steamer trunk, a pile of wood for the stove, and an enormous galvanized-metal washtub with foodstuffs—dried beans, hams, and some canned goods—carefully stacked inside.

She was mulling it all over when Bandit and Mutt returned. Bandit was carrying a big armload of firewood. "Just in time, I see," he said when he saw Louisa huddling by the near-dead stove. He was dressed only in an undershirt, trousers, and his suspenders. He grinned at her shocked expression—it had to be well below zero outside, not counting the effect of the bracing wind.

"There's an old saying that wood warms you twice," he said. "Once when you split it, and a second time when you burn it."

He opened the woodstove and shoved in a few lengths. "You'll be warm again soon. It's like this every morning in the winter—sometimes cold enough that the water in the coffee pot is frozen, but in under an hour the cabin is nice and warm."

"You must have built it well," she said.

"I made my fair share of mistakes, believe me," he replied, stirring the fire with a poker. "But I learned from them, and fixed them one by one. Now the whole place is very snug. You'll see, it gets like a sweat lodge in here once that fire gets going."

Louisa gave him a wan smile. "So on top of being stranded, I have *that* to look forward to. Sweating all winter."

"Now, now, Miss MacGregor. It's not so bad as all that. Look on the bright side—you're stranded, true, but you are stranded in some of the most beautiful wilderness in the world. Soon I'll give you a little tour, and you'll see it for yourself."

"Hmm," she said, warming her hands in front of the stove. "I rather think Central Park is quite wild enough for my taste."

He sat down on the edge of the bed, his blue eyes sparkling and his face ruddy with the cold. "You never know . . . your opinion may change in time."

The stove was crackling in earnest now, and shimmering waves of heat were rising from its grey iron. The cabin was quickly becoming cozy again.

"Dare I ask what I have been missing back in the big wide world?" Bandit said. "I will admit I've been a little bit curious. It's been quite a while since I've had any news at all."

Louisa folded her arms across her chest. "Well, let me think. We had a war with Spain last year."

"I'm not a *hermit*," he said, rolling his eyes. "I *do* venture into civilization, or what passes for it in these parts, when the weather's good."

"How would *I* know what someone like *you* does all year?" she said, still peeved at him and by the idea of being trapped in this cabin—however clean, tidy, and now warm—for months.

He laughed. He had a really engaging laugh, rich and sonorous. "*Someone like me*," he repeated. "How many other people like me do you know?"

"None, I assure you. Thankfully."

"Then on with the news!" he said, unfazed.

"Former President Grant's granddaughter Julia married a Russian prince last month."

"There's a lot of that going around."

"A lot of what? Marriage?"

"Yes, that, but I meant young American ladies marrying foreign nobility."

"Can you blame them?" Louisa said. "I suppose you think that such promising, well-bred young ladies as Miss Grant ought to marry mountain men instead of princes."

"You might be surprised, you know. Some mountain men might make very good husbands."

"Well, don't get any ideas."

"I won't. My point is simply that money and a title don't make a man a good husband."

"Perhaps not, but they're a good start."

"Ah, Miss MacGregor, if you only knew."

She shot him a sharp glance. "I beg your pardon! I'll have you know, Your Highness, that New York society *is* something I know rather well. My father is a *judge*, and we live on Fifth Avenue."

"That is very impressive," Bandit said.

"Yes it is. And among the many things you don't know about me is that I was recently engaged to a young man whose family is among the Four Hundred."

"The four hundred people who matter in New York," he said.

"*You* know about the Four Hundred?"

"I *do* know a thing or two," he replied. "Mr. Ward McAllister is the fellow who kept the list. And Mrs. Astor is at the top, of course."

Louisa looked surprised. "Well done," she said slowly. "You're more up-to-date than I expected."

"Now Lou—"

"Louisa."

He ignored her. "Since you brought it up—I have a question for you. While I have no doubt that your father is a highly esteemed member of the bench, and your family a very good one indeed . . . if you don't mind my saying, the Four Hundred is the most difficult club in New York to join. In fact, generally speaking, one *cannot* join. One is either born into it, or consigned forever to outer darkness."

"What are you scratching at?"

"Nothing, really."

Louisa reddened. "Oh, you're scratching at *something*," she said. "Why don't you just come out and say it?"

He cleared his throat. "Well, then . . . if you insist. To be honest, I'm a bit surprised that such a distinguished family as your fiancé's has permitted him to enter into an engagement with a young lady outside their set."

Her face deepened to crimson. "And how would *you* know that *my* family is not among the Four Hundred? Do you know everyone in the Four Hundred?"

"Of course not."

"Then perhaps you might keep your conjectures in better check."

He sat on the edge of the bed, his fingers in a steeple between his legs.

"May I ask when your nuptials are scheduled?" he said after a long and frosty silence.

"I don't want to talk about it anymore," Louisa said. "It's none of your concern."

"Is it wrong to want to know a little bit about the woman who is sharing my bed?"

"I am not *sharing your bed*, sir!" she snapped. "Even a man of *your* class must know that such a thing is simply not said. I deeply resent any implic—"

Bandit threw back his head and laughed heartily. "Lou, you are a most enthralling creature! You don't know any more about me than I know about you. And yet I'm the only one of us curious about the other."

"As I suggested a moment ago, a little *less* curiosity would be rather welcome."

He slapped his hands on his thighs and stood. "Very well, then! I have some little repairs that are calling my name, so if you'll excuse me, I'll leave you in peace. Thank you for sharing the news of the day with me." He paused. "And naturally, please accept my best wishes on your coming marriage. Even if not to a prince of the blood, wedding a member of the Four Hundred is the next best thing."

Bandit went to the far side of the cabin and picked up a hammer, a coil of oakum, and some nails. He began to pound the oakum into a number of cracks that the cold had opened between the window frames and the log walls.

He was tapping steadily away when Lou, staring into the blazing woodstove, spoke again.

"Our engagement was called off," she said quietly. "Since you're so *curious*."

Bandit put down his hammer and walked back over to the stove. He sat down on the edge of the bed. "I am sorry to hear that," he said.

She looked away and quickly wiped her cheek with the back of her hand. "I suppose it wasn't meant to be, that's all. Life goes on."

He looked down into his lap. "Yes, it does," he said, almost to himself. "But it doesn't mean that the things that happen along the way can't cause us terrible pain."

Louisa began to weep softly. "I miss him, that's all," she said, her voice catching.

"Of course you do," Bandit said. "He was to be your husband."

She wiped her eyes again and nodded. "How mortifying," she mumbled. "Blubbering like a schoolgirl in front of some strange mountain man."

"I'm not so very strange, Lou. And I know what it feels like to hurt."

She looked over at him, tears running down her cheeks at such a pace she couldn't wipe them away. "Not like *this*, you don't," she sobbed. "*And my name's not Lou!*"

Bandit got up, fetched a clean rag from the rag bucket and brought it over to her. "Here," he said, kneeling next to her chair.

She dried her eyes, blew her nose with a loud honk, and composed herself. "I really must apologize," she said. "I can assure you that will be the final display of its kind."

"Don't say that," Bandit replied. "It's good to cry. When the sky becomes too full, what does it do? It rains, and sometimes violently. But afterward, it's clear and blue again."

Lou blew her nose again. "That is most gracious of you," she sniffled. "I do feel a little better."

He smiled at her. "Good. Now I have found that after a good cry, the best thing to do is to get busy with something else entirely and let things settle. So how would you like to help me finish stuffing oakum around the windows?"

"I don't know how."

He clapped his big hands. "Why, Miss MacGregor! The things you've missed out on! But take heart—soon you will learn something new and useful. You never know, one day you may have to stuff some oakum around the windows of your family's place on Fifth Avenue."

She couldn't help but smile.

6

The Tunnel

Stuffing oakum wasn't difficult, but like every skill it took a little practice to do it well. Bandit had been right: After her cry, and getting busy with a chore, she had felt better than she had in a very long time. The High Sierra, the cabin, and this philosophical mountain man were worlds apart from anything she had ever known, and simply learning how to live with each of them allowed precious little room in her mind for other, more troubling thoughts.

It snowed and snowed and snowed the entire day, and it was still snowing without letup when the sun at last gave up and sagged behind the peaks. Their second night together followed the first night's pattern, except that this time Mutt had to clamber over a three-foot-high wall of snow when Bandit opened the cabin door to take him out.

Then they had fallen asleep next to each other again, the wind howling a gale in the high, hidden valley, but Bandit's sturdy little cabin—with their fresh oakum around its window frames—held firm and tight.

When Louisa awoke again, though, the bed felt cold, and she felt a flush of fear that perhaps her rescuer had given up on her and fled. She sat bolt upright and was relieved to find him still clad in his union suit, busily reviving the fire in the woodstove.

"Well, good morning, Lou," he said cheerfully. "You can go back to sleep if you like."

"Is it morning already?" she asked, rubbing her eyes. "It's still so dark."

"Ha! That's because we're snowed under. Buried up to the eaves, at least."

"Are you serious?"

"Entirely. That blizzard kept blowing most of the night. Didn't you hear it?"

She had to admit to herself that she'd slept very soundly next to the big lump. "No, I didn't," she said without thinking. "I . . . I must have been exhausted."

"Then why don't you stay put and relax while the fire gets going, and I'll make us some coffee?"

She shivered. "It's cold under here, too. I might as well get up."

"Nothing doing," he said. "You need your rest." With that, he slid back under the blankets with her. He lay on his back, hands folded over his stomach.

They lay there for a few minutes, and soon the bed was warm again.

"What should we do now?" she asked.

He looked over at her and cocked an eyebrow. "Hmm. Do you have something special in mind?"

"Don't be a pig."

"Oink," he said.

"Juvenile. What I *meant* was what do we do if the cabin is snowed under? How do we get out?"

"Mostly, we don't," he said. "But I *will* have to clear the snow away from the chimney. If it gets plugged up, this place will fill with smoke in minutes. Fortunately I do have a few tricks up my sleeve for such occasions—but since it is still drawing now, there's no particular hurry."

"Oh good," she said, despite herself. She felt herself falling into a deep place as sleep stole over her again.

When she again opened her eyes, the cabin was warm and comfortable. Bandit was now sitting on his chair, sewing together what looked like large, irregular pieces of tanned pelts, leather side out.

"I'll bet you haven't slept this well at the Waldorf," he said sidelong.

"I'm tired, that's all," she said, bleary-eyed. "What are you doing?"

He nodded toward her velvet traveling suit, neatly hanging on a peg under the rafters. "You can't very well be a mountain lady wearing *that* getup. So I've made you a pair of trousers out of deerskin—by estimating your size, naturally."

"You're back to this, are you? Is my physique some kind of obsession with you?"

"I don't think so—but if I had a tailor's tape, would you let me take your measurements?"

"I most certainly would *not*."

"Then I must estimate, or obsess if you prefer. Either way, you now have some proper trousers, and I have a spare work shirt that will serve as a blouse. I cut down one of my old belts to fit you, too. Just put it around the work shirt and fasten it over your trousers."

"I'll look quite a sight," she said. "Not that anyone will see me, though."

"*I'll* see you. Doesn't that count?"

"You say the oddest things," she said. "I suppose I ought to thank you, though."

"And you are very welcome. Now . . . those dainty little shoes of yours are another problem. They're not durable, and your feet will freeze in them. So I've also very nearly finished making you a very nice pair of moccasins, lined with warm fur."

"My," she said. "I'll look like a wild Indian."

His eyes sparkled at her in the firelight. "That's who taught me to sew, you know," he said, holding up his needle. "The local Indians."

She looked horrified. "You know *Indians*? Aren't you scared to death of them?"

"Why should I be?"

"Because Indians hate the white man!"

He looked back down at his work. "Let me tell you something about Indians," he said. "They don't like people who lie, and they don't like people who steal. And that's pretty much all that white folks have done to them for generations. So while some Indians do hate white people, at least they have a reason to. Believe me, plenty of white folks hate Indians for no reason at all."

"Mind you, I don't care to be lied to or stolen from, either. But still! Weren't you afraid that they'd turn on you?"

"Lots of people will turn on you," he replied, pushing his awl through the leather. "Regardless of the color of their skin."

"Now *that* I can't argue with," she said, almost to herself. "Nevertheless, I hope I won't encounter any Indians during my sojourn here."

"*Sojourn*," he repeated. "You're funny. *Sojourn*."

"It means a short stay."

"I know what it means. I just haven't heard that word since I left New York. It takes me back." He held out the trousers. "Voilà!" he said, tossing them on the bed along with the denim work shirt and the belt. "Go ahead—try 'em on."

She looked around. "If you insist. Where may I change in privacy?"

"My, how perfectly dreadful!" he said in a high-pitched voice, clutching at imaginary pearls. "I seem to have entirely forgotten to install changing facilities at my estate!"

"How very droll. The sheer indignity of—"

"Oh, don't be so dramatic. You may change right where you are. I'll simply look away."

"Dramatic? This is horrendous. Given your apparent obsession with my physique, I don't believe for a moment that you'll 'simply look away.' No sir, nothing doing. You will *turn around*—and you'd better not turn back until I tell you to." She twirled a finger in the air.

He swiveled his chair around and began to hum some brisk tune that had been popular several years before.

She hurriedly pulled her nightdress over her head and buttoned up the denim work shirt, which was old and soft but huge on her. The trousers fit surprisingly well, though, and when she secured the belt over the tails of the shirt, Louisa had to admit to herself that the whole ensemble looked rather daring, in an Annie Oakley sort of way.

"You may turn around now," she said.

Bandit turned, looked her over, and whistled softly. "Lou, we may just make a mountain lady out of you after all. How's the fit? Everything comfortable?"

She wriggled around a moment inside her new garments. "Not bad, though I could benefit from a chemise under the shirt. And the trousers tickle a little."

"Both easily addressed," he replied. "I'll make you an undershirt out of an old bedsheet. You may call it a *chemise* if you like, however. And so far as the tickling goes, if you'll give me your trousers again, I can cut the fur away from your private parts."

Lou blushed to the roots of her hair. "I didn't mean to imply that it tickled *there*," she said in horror. "I meant the *legs*."

"Ah! That's a relief. I suppose I assumed—"

"Well, don't assume. In case no one has ever told you, you have a dirty mind."

"And you have ticklish legs. Now since you're all dressed up, have some of that deer meat while I finish stitching your moccasins. And then I have something very interesting to show you."

THIS TIME, LOU COULDN'T deny that she was hungry and, to her great surprise, found fried venison to be nowhere near as awful as she'd feared. Actually, it was rather satisfying. While she ate, Bandit finished up her moccasins and picked up his book again.

"How was your breakfast?" he asked when she had finished.

"Really quite tasty. I rather liked it, I must admit. And the coffee . . . well, I've already praised your coffee."

"It never hurts to compliment a chef twice, especially since you had at least two cups."

"Don't be stingy."

"I'm not stingy—just fishing for compliments. Now try on your new moccasins, and we'll get some fresh air and I'll dig us out. The wind's died down, so I'm thinking this storm's behind us."

"I'll try them on directly," she said, "but before I do . . . I don't quite know how to say this . . ."

"You have to use the pot."

She covered her face with her hands. "Yes," she mumbled through them.

"Speaking of fresh air," he said with a smirk.

"That is simply crude."

"Just trying to lighten the mood, Lou. I'll turn around again. Take the pot over to the corner and do whatever you have to do."

From the far end of the cabin, he heard her remove the china lid from the pot and rustle around a bit, then a telltale sound.

"How utterly mortifying," he heard her say under her breath.

"There's a stack of paper next to the washtub," he called over his shoulder.

"I see it," she said quietly, and after another minute he heard her replace the lid. When he turned around again he found her with her face in her hands again, weeping.

"Oh, Lou, it's all right," he said, walking over and perching atop the big steamer trunk. "I don't mind. I'm just an old mountain man all by himself up here."

"You're not *old*," she sniffled. "You can't be more than thirty-five, and if that dreadful beard of yours were gone, you'd could pass for thirty."

"I'm thirty-one," he said. "And if you like, I'll shave off the beard."

With her heel, she pushed the chamber pot away. "I need to empty this."

"And that's one of the reasons we're leaving the cabin."

He stepped to the center of the room, lifted a corner of the big Oriental rug and pulled it aside. Under it, recessed into the planking, was what looked to be a big trapdoor.

"Abracadabra," Bandit said, turning an iron ring and pulling upward. Sure enough, a trapdoor swung open on hidden hinges that allowed it to lie flush with the floor.

He took down a railroad lantern from a peg and lit it with a splinter of wood he put into the fire. "Hold this, if you would," he said, handing her the lantern.

They looked down into the trapdoor opening and saw a short ladder angled against the bedrock below. He descended the ladder, carrying the chamber pot, and at the bottom gestured for her to hand down the lantern and join him. She complied, her fur pants tickling as she descended.

At the bottom, she looked around and saw that they were standing in a tunnel, its ceiling a little taller than Bandit, hung with icicles, and braced with big wooden beams. It stretched away into darkness.

"I built my cabin over an old mine," he said. "I use these tunnels for storing things, and they would come in very handy if, heaven forbid, we ever had to escape from a fire or too much smoke. And when we're snowed under . . . well, you're about to see another way they can be useful."

7

In My Shoes

Judge James J. MacGregor's full face was red and contorted with rage. "I simply cannot understand what in *thunder* could have possessed you to leave my daughter—"

"As I have been *trying* to explain, Your Honor," said Niles Bartholomew, president of the Sierra Pacific Railroad, "our engineer reported that his conductor found your palace car locked up tight, and that there was no reply to his continued attempts to elicit any response from within."

"That doesn't mean my daughter wasn't inside it, you buffoon!" roared the judge. "And your engineer took off and left her stranded in—oh, I can't even bear to say it. What's more, my son had to telephone me long-distance when his sister did not alight, as expected, from what was left of her train. Your so-called engineer hadn't even the decency to call me himself!"

"Judge MacGregor," the railroad baron said, "do note that *I* called you personally the instant I heard the unfortunate news. Surely you can understand that absent any response from inside your private car, and facing the prospect that an entire train full of passengers and crew might be lost, my engineer had no other option but to depart. Before it was too late."

"You'll regret this, Bartholomew," the jurist snarled, jabbing his finger in the man's face. "My daughter is very probably dead already, either of exposure or privation. I insist that you send a special train immediately—if you haven't already—to effect a rescue. And you may expect that I will be on board, sir."

Bartholomew shook his head sadly. "Your Honor, I wish that I could give you a different answer. But I'm afraid you are asking the impossible. Our tracks are closed almost as far back as the Nevada border. No one in our lifetimes has seen such a storm—why, everyone in my operation has told me that it's the worst since the winter of '46."

"1846 was a long time ago," the judge said. "You'd think your railroad might have learned a thing or two in half a century."

"We have, and ours is the safest line in that unforgiving region. But ultimately, no one is more powerful than the Sierras themselves. And, with all respect—and as much as it pains me to say this—surely you recall that it was *you* who entreated me, and at the last minute, to add your car to this train. Under any circumstances but your own direct insistence, I would *never* have allowed a private car on the last train of the season. The risk is too great—as I stated *quite* clearly at the time."

"It's one thing to tell me there's a risk, and quite another to have no plan to deal with it if the worst happens," the judge growled. "Now when *can* we get a rescue mission under way?"

"Late March, if the weather cooperates," the railroad man said. "Otherwise, April. There is no prospect of getting to the—"

The judge held up his hand. "If you please, sir, do not utter the name of that horrible place in my presence. I won't hear it."

"I understand. But I must reiterate that there is no prospect of getting anywhere near it until the spring thaw. It's the Sierra Nevada mountains, Your Honor. Only God himself—"

"—can save my daughter now. Isn't that what you are saying?"

"I was going to say, can traverse such country in the depths of winter."

"You might as well have said the one as the other," Judge MacGregor said more gently. "Bartholomew, I ask you to put yourself in my shoes for a moment. Louisa is my only daughter, and I love her dearly. You, like every other soul in New York City, know all too well that she has endured difficult times of late. And now, instead of enjoying a restorative change of scenery, she is . . . freezing or starving to death inside my own private rail car! It's more than any man can bear."

Bartholomew studied the top of his desk. "Judge MacGregor," he said softly, "I am also a father. And I assure you that in your shoes I would feel very much the same as you do. All I would ask, sir, is for you to put yourself also in mine. My crew, and ultimately myself, had two hundred lives in our care on that train. The loss of any one of them is a tragedy, but the loss of two hundred would be catastrophic."

The judge fixed his keen eyes on the railroad man and nodded. "I sit behind a bench every day of my life, weighing good against evil, and making difficult choices between one person's rights and another's. And to be justice at all, justice must wear a blindfold, whether in the courtroom or in running a railroad. So I assure you that I do understand your position, however distressing I may find it personally."

"Thank you for that, sir," Bartholomew said. "I give you my word of honor that, at the earliest opportunity after the thaw, we will mount a search party for your daughter."

"Then tell it to me straight out. Exactly what is my daughter facing until that time? And what do you think are her chances?"

The railroad man sighed. "Survival in the Sierras is a matter of adequate food, shelter, and warmth," he said. "Your daughter has excellent shelter, fortunately. If she can recover some of the coal jettisoned from the train, she would easily have sufficient fuel to keep her stove going. While the baggage car contains more than enough food to last the winter, I must observe that such cars are kept securely locked. She would have to break in somehow."

There was a long pause before the judge spoke again. "Thank you for your honesty, sir," he said. "It appears all we can do is pray for a miracle."

"Miracles do happen," Bartholomew said.

"Humpf. Not very often, they don't."

"That's what makes them miracles, Your Honor."

8

Into the High Sierra

*L*eaning against the tunnel wall were a pair of snowshoes and a shovel with a long handle. Bandit put the snowshoes under one arm and threw the shovel over his shoulder.

"Come, Mutt!" he yelled up through the trapdoor opening, and in seconds the huge dog came hurtling down from above, landing with surprising grace on the floor of the tunnel.

Bandit turned and gestured with his head. "Right this way, Miss."

The tunnel had been roughly hewn out of the living rock, and by the flickering light of the railroad lantern, Lou looked up nervously to see if the ceiling seemed solid and well-braced. They had gone about ten yards when Bandit thrust out his pair of snowshoes, and Lou ran smack into them.

"Ouch!" she said. "What in the world was *that* for?"

"You can't sleepwalk in the Sierras," he said with a frown. "You're staring at the ceiling the whole time and not looking where you're putting your feet."

"It may not seem reasonable to you, but I'm afraid we'll be buried alive!"

"May be a blessing in disguise," he muttered.

"That is entirely uncalled for. I am doing the best I can!"

His face softened. "I know you are. But you really do have to pay attention out here, not just bumble along."

"You just can't let anything go, can you? *Bumbling*?"

"If you're not bumbling, then tell me what's three steps ahead on the right."

"How would I know?"

"You would know if you had been paying attention. If you were down here alone, and someday you might have to be, you'd have bumbled into *that*." He pointed just ahead.

On the right side of the tunnel was a three-foot square hole, brimful of blackness and leading to God knows where.

"What in the world is that?" Lou asked.

"It's a vertical shaft, straight down. I don't know how far down it goes, but far. If you had blundered into that, you'd be a goner."

She put her hands on her hips. "Who in his right mind puts a bottomless pit by the side of a pathway?"

"Um, miners do," Bandit said. "It's a *mine*."

"I know *that*."

"Well, you might also care to know that if you went down in that hole, even if you weren't killed by the fall, you'd have a big surprise waiting for you at the bottom."

"What kind of surprise?"

He removed the lid from the chamber pot and upended it, dumping the contents into the hole. "This is where I empty the solids," he said. "At the bottom, it's probably at least three feet deep in—"

"Disgusting," she said, looking away as the mouth of the shaft belched forth a distant *splat*. "There is no need to elaborate further. I take your point."

He laughed and set down the empty pot. "Now follow along. But keep your eyes peeled this time."

They had walked another fifty yards or so, when the tunnel widened out into a small, domed cave.

"See? This is how we get out when we're snowed under," he said. "From here I can snowshoe over to the cabin and dig the place out."

They stepped out from under the overhanging eaves of the cave and into a sparkling wonderland. Protected from wind by the roots of the mountains themselves, the cave was dry, bare rock—but just beyond its opening extended a vast wilderness of snow. Everywhere snow!— more snow than Louisa had ever imagined existed—heaving swells of it undulating ten and twenty feet above the valley floor, and, poking like lighthouses above them, scattered, icy pillars of the stuff, which the wild wind had carved into fantastic shapes. On the steep slopes embracing the valley, even the loftiest lodgepoles had been transformed into topiaries of the whitest meringue.

And above this empire of snow loomed the soaring Sierras, an impregnable fortress of rock and ice roofed by an endless azure sky. In the high, hidden valley all was quiet—the quietest place Louisa had ever been—with only the soft *whoosh* of the wind and the rippling of the bright stream to test the eternal silence of the high country.

"Oh *my*," she gasped, and stopped. She bent over suddenly, clutching her chest.

He placed his hand on her back. "Don't worry—it's normal," he said. "Take some deep breaths. The air is very thin up here—before long, you'll get used to it."

She caught her breath at last and stood up. Tears were coursing down her cheeks.

"What's wrong?"

"It w-wasn't the altitude," she stammered, her lip quivering. "It was something different—in *here*." She placed her hand over her heart.

A look of concern crossed his face. "Maybe we had better—"

"No," she said. "I'm sorry. I didn't mean to frighten you. It's hard to describe, but . . ."

"But what? You need to tell me if you're unwell."

"I'm fine, truly I am. It wasn't a bad feeling—in fact, it was wonderful. Just—odd."

"Will you tell me what it was?"

"I would if I knew a word for it," Lou said. "I'm sure this will sound silly, but oh well . . . I felt—no, I *knew*—that I had stepped into the presence of God himself. And . . . how very small I am, and how very *great*—" She turned away, again overcome.

"That's *far* from being silly," Bandit said softly. "It's beautiful and holy. And there *is* a word for it—*reverence*."

She nodded and dried her eyes on her sleeve. "I'll never forget this moment so long as I live," she said, her voice quavering.

They stood in silence for long minutes, quietly bathing in the wild serenity of their hidden valley.

"As much as I'd love to stay here," he said at last, "I really should get on my way before the chimney plugs up."

"Don't go!" she blurted, then caught herself. "I mean to say, I wish you hadn't such a difficult task to attend to."

"It's not so bad. Fortunately, the cabin is only a hundred yards or so around the bend of the creek. It won't take me long at all."

"May I come with you?"

"I wish you could, but you don't have any snowshoes yet. Until I make you a pair, you mustn't venture out on the snow, or—*poof!*—you'll disappear forever. So this time, wait here, and I'll hoof it over to the cabin. I'll be back in no time." He began lashing on his snowshoes.

"Oh my," she said, feeling a wash of fear. "I shouldn't like to stay here alone. What if one of those awful grizzly bears happens by?"

"There haven't been any grizzlies seen around here for some time,"

Bandit said. "Sad to say, they were hunted into extinction. Only black bears remain nowadays."

"Grizzly bears, black bears—I shouldn't like to encounter either of them."

"You won't—or not for a few months, at least. They're hibernating now, sleeping away the winter. And Mutt will stay here with you, so you'll be quite safe while you take in this marvelous view. Now—and I don't mean to rattle you—unexpected things can and do happen out here, even to someone with experience. So if I'm not back in an hour, I want you to go back through the tunnel and to the cabin."

"You're frightening me," she said. "*Please* don't go if something might happen to you!"

"I predict I'll be fine. But one of these days, you may have to fend for yourself—and I want to make sure that I teach you how, should that time ever come."

She looked down at her feet, clad in her pretty new moccasins with their fur trimmings, feeling unexpectedly proud of them and wanting to put them up next to the woodstove back in the cozy little cabin. *Now be brave, Louisa MacGregor,* she said to herself. *You can manage this.*

"Then I'll stay here with Mutt, and do as you say."

"Now that's the spirit! Mutt, you stay here with Lou." The dog barked and sat down next to Louisa, and Bandit winked at them. Then he turned and began walking with his peculiar, shuffling snowshoe gait over the tops of the drifts.

She patted Mutt's flat head, feeling reassured that the big, strong dog was sitting next to her, and watched Bandit's great buffalo robe disappear around the bend in the creek. He had been gone for only a minute or two when she began to regret having told him about her unusual feeling.

What is *wrong* with me? she thought. Going on about *the presence of God*? He must think I'm *insane*. Why can't I ever just keep my mouth shut?

He was away only about three-quarters of an hour before she saw him come around the bend, trudging resolutely toward her. The sun had now cleared the treetops, and the white landscape was becoming painfully bright, so bright that she had to retreat into the soothing dusk of the cave.

"We're all dug out!" he said, taking off his snowshoes and stamping up to her. "Everything been all right here, I hope?" He had donned some kind of smoked glasses, presumably to guard against the harsh glare.

"Mutt and I held the fort well enough, I should think."

"As I knew you would. Have you been enjoying the scenery?"

"Yes indeed. And by the way—I believe you were right about the thin air, after all. I sure was having some queer thoughts until I caught my breath. So I sincerely hope you'll forgive me for babbling on as I did. I'm really quite ashamed of myself."

He took off his smoked glasses and looked at her so strangely that she drew a sharp little breath.

"Ashamed?"

"Yes, though I *am* grateful for your concern."

He put on his spectacles again, the blue eyes disappearing into black. "And here I was just beginning to think that I might have gotten you all wrong."

"What in the *world* is that supposed to mean?"

"Don't trouble yourself about it. Just one of my own occasional queer thoughts."

"You've lost me entirely," she said. "May we please return to the cabin now?"

"Homesick already?"

"My *home* is in Manhattan."

He rolled his eyes. "How could I forget?"

"Don't always be such a smart aleck. And don't imagine *I've* forgotten that you may be nothing more than an outlaw bent on ravishing young ladies stranded in the snow."

She turned on her heel and began walking crisply back into the tunnel. This time, she watched her feet as they walked, not so much to avoid falling into a disused mineshaft, but rather to keep the pretty new moccasins from getting any dirtier than they had to.

He caught her up in a step or two. "There's that *ravishment* stuff again. Why in the world would I want to ravish you?"

"And why wouldn't you? A big, strapping man brooding out here in the trackless wilderness without any human companionship, and suddenly a beautiful damsel in distress falls into his clutches? Why, it's like any number of fairy tales."

He listened as they walked. "Is that the way you see all this? Truly?"

"Why yes, I suppose that I do."

"Well then, I don't mind saying that your fairy tale says more about you than it does about me."

"How so, smart aleck?"

"Because I see this story as that of a young man who likes his solitude, living in peace with his dog and his cat and all of nature, and because he succumbed to curiosity and investigated a stranded train—which by the way might have stranded *anywhere else* but near his home—he acquired a rich, persnickety city girl whom he must now look after until he can load her onto the first spring train."

She stopped and glared over at him in the gloom. "That is without a doubt the nastiest thing anyone's ever said to me."

"It's merely an alternative storyline, my dear."

"I am not your *dear*, ravisher. And I'm *not* a 'rich, persnickety city girl,' either. Why, look at how quickly I've taken to my new wardrobe."

"Yes," he said wryly, "while trying not to get your moccasins wet."

She blushed, thankful for the darkness of the tunnel. "They're *new*. I should like to keep them nice."

"So let me analyze this a moment," Bandit said as the tunnel began to slope upward. "You travel in a . . . oh, what's the word? . . . yes, that's it! . . . in an *opulent* palace car. That makes you *rich*. You are from New York, which is most definitely a *city*, and a very big one at that. And I hardly think it necessary to offer evidence of your *persnicketiness*. So there it is. Rich. Persnickety. City girl."

"And you're a surly, mean mountain man."

"Why do you think I'm better off on my own?"

They arrived at the ladder, and Bandit gathered up Mutt in his arms as easily as if the giant dog were still a puppy. He scaled the ladder, let Mutt loose in the cabin, and turned and held out his hand to Louisa, who was standing uneasily in the tunnel. "Come on up," he said. "I'll make us something to eat."

She crossed her arms and shook her head. "I don't feel welcome here anymore."

"Now don't be that way. You'll catch your death down there."

"I don't care. I don't want to see your ugly face ever again."

"I've been called a lot of things in my time, but never *ugly*. And just when I was thinking about shaving off my beard, too."

Lou tried to suppress a smile.

"Come on now, dear," Bandit said. "Let's let bygones be bygones."

"How many times do I have to say it? I am *not* your dear."

"All right. I'm not going to try to change your mind if you've made it up. But if you're going to stay down there for the winter, at least bring the chamber pot up before bedtime."

He hopped out of the trapdoor opening, and she heard his boots thud across the planks toward the cheery woodstove and their cozy bed. *His bed*, she corrected herself.

She stood in the tunnel for a few minutes, at a loss for what to do next. Soon she could smell coffee again, and this time the toothsome scent of frying bacon. Lou was hungry, and getting cold, and her pretty moccasins were wet clear through. Quietly she climbed the ladder and crawled out into the warm cabin, where Bandit was tending the stove. He looked over his shoulder as she hauled herself out of the opening, clutching the chamber pot under one arm.

"I thought you never wanted to see me again," he said.

"I don't, but you asked me to bring the chamber pot back."

"Well, if you've decided to stay aboveground, at least close the trapdoor. You were letting in a cold draft the whole time you were down there."

She closed the trapdoor and took off her moccasins. "My new shoes got wet," she said disconsolately, dangling them from one hand.

"Then come on over here and we'll get them nice and dry by the stove. And we'll get you all warmed up in the process. To top it off, I'll even let you have the chair."

Louisa gave a little snort. She walked over, plopped down on the chair, and put her cold feet as near the hot stove as she dared. Bandit took the wet moccasins from her and set them on a little footstool to dry. He handed her a mug of steaming coffee.

"Would you have really let me die down there?" she asked after a moment. "If you didn't need the chamber pot again, that is."

"What do you think?"

"I couldn't possibly say. You're a bit of a paradox. Sometimes you seem like a very kind person, and other times you seem like a mean old ogre."

He chuckled, turning the bacon in the sizzling fat. "I suppose I am both of those things. But then again, you seem sometimes like a wise and sensitive woman, and at others like a persnickety city girl."

"Oooh, you," she muttered into her coffee.

9

The Sleeping Draught

"Scoot *out*, you big lump," she said to Bandit an hour after they'd turned in, nudging him with an elbow. "I have to use the conveniences."

"Convenient for *whom*?" he mumbled, half-asleep. He threw his legs over the side of the bed and sat up so that Lou could crawl past. She took the thunder mug from under the bed and walked quietly over to the other end of the cabin.

"Lie back down," she said over her shoulder. "And face away."

He obliged, and she emptied her bladder into the pot. Lou replaced the lid and as she was about to return to bed, felt a familiar urge. She opened her carpetbag and fumbled around in it until her hand touched the familiar bottle. Pulling out its tiny cork, she put the bottle's mouth against hers.

"What in the world is *that*?" came his voice from behind her. She stoppered the bottle quickly and tucked it back into her bag.

"What in the world is *what*? I was using the facilities."

"I know. I'm not deaf. I mean *after* that. You drank something."

"You are a nosy thing, aren't you? You were supposed to be looking away."

"I was, until I heard you swallow. What was it?" He struck a lucifer with his thumbnail and lit the bedside candle. His face looked worried in the wavering light.

"It's none of your business. Go back to sleep."

Instead, he took up the candlestick and strode across the cabin. Pushing past her, he opened up her carpetbag and fished around inside. He found the bottle and held it up to the candle.

"*Laudanum?*" he said. "Really?"

She was already beginning to feel relaxed as the warm rush of opium swirled around her bloodstream. "What of it? Laudanum is perfectly legal."

"It doesn't matter to me if it's *legal*. It's dangerous," he said, shaking the bottle. "I've known people who have become slaves to this stuff."

"Not me. I'm no one's slave."

"And that's what they all say. Why are you taking this?"

"Who are you, the Pinkertons? I don't owe you any answers about my personal business."

"You do if you're living with me," Bandit said. "I don't plan to be tending a narcotics addict all winter. We'll have more than enough challenges as it is."

"I'm not an *addict,*" she protested, weaving on her feet. "Now give me that back." She snatched the bottle from his hand and clasped it against her body. "And if you'll only get out of my way, I'd like to get back into bed now. I'm getting cold out here."

"You must know we'll be talking about this in the morning."

"Yeah, yeah. Big man with the big voice. You're worse than my father." She shoved him aside and stumbled over to the bed, still clutching her bottle. She climbed back under the covers, turned her face to the wall, and was soon snoring lustily.

IN THE MORNING, LOUISA woke with an electric jolt of fear, momentarily worried that Bandit might have dumped her laudanum out into the snow. To her relief, she found the bottle still in bed next to her, shy only of the swallow she'd taken the previous night. Bandit was sitting on his chair, nursing a mug of coffee and staring into the stove.

She slid out, put her bottle away in her carpetbag, and then returned to sit on the edge of the bed. Without a word, Bandit handed her a mug of coffee.

"Thank you," she said.

"Don't mention it."

"*Well?*" she said after a minute of strained silence. "Go on. I know you can hardly wait."

He leveled his gaze at her. "First, and for the record," he said, "I am most definitely *not* your father. And thank God for that, because that poor man has a heavy cross to bear."

"You're just being insulting."

"Perhaps, but I don't think I'm far off. I can recognize when some-one's been coddled, Lou. But while fathers can do that with their daughters, please do not expect it from *me*."

"Coddling, as you call it, is neither necessary nor desired. And especially not from *you*."

"Hmm. Then here's what I think, without any coddling. I think you've developed quite a substantial tolerance for your little tipple. The amount you downed last evening—without much effect, I may add—could have killed a bull elephant. Maybe two. So what's the story?"

"There's no *story*. It's a doctor's prescription. I had my appendix removed three years ago, and he prescribed it for the pain."

"*Three years ago?* And you're still taking it? Sorry, but that makes you an *addict*, Lou."

"Nonsense."

"Be that as it may, I don't want you to take any more of it."

"What do you care? You haven't any idea of what my life has been like. And if sometimes I need to forget—"

"You're far too young to have so many bad memories. You can't be more than twenty-five."

"I am not engaging in any discussions about my age, nor about my weight, nor about my physique, as you have attempted to do so often already. Pry, pry, pry. That's all you do."

"Then if you insist on poisoning yourself, do us both a favor and wander out in the snow someplace first, because I don't want you getting high under my roof. I've seen what that drug can do, and it nauseates me."

"Your cabin, your rules, is that it? Ha! You do sound rather like my father, after all."

His face softened. "Lou, all I'm saying is that . . . for physical pain, laudanum and all the rest are a godsend. But for the kind of pain you've suffered . . . the only cure for that is *time*."

"I'll have to think about that," she said, and poured herself more coffee. "Now before you can resume lecturing me about my personal affairs, may I inquire as to where precisely we are?"

"Don't think for a minute that I can't tell you're trying to change the subject."

"Oh, I'm sure you'll snap back to it eventually, as you do about my physique. But before you do, I think I have a right to know where you are holding me hostage."

He put his face into his hands for a moment. "*Hostage*," he mumbled, and looked up at her again. "Fine. Have you heard of the Donner Party?"

"Of course I've heard of the Donner Party! If you can't tell, I've had an excellent education."

"I *could* tell. But I knew it was only a matter of time until you made it explicit."

"What is that supposed to mean?"

"Nothing at all. In any case, your palace car is at present stranded in the Donner Pass. Very near the place where the Donner Party were themselves stranded, with such unfortunate consequences."

"More good news," she said. "You'll probably end up eating me."

He snickered. "Good gracious me! Even for a city girl, you do move *fast*."

She blushed. "That is a perfectly *vile* thing to say. You are a filthy, filthy man."

"Laugh a little, sourpuss," he said. "Cannibalism aside, right now you're only a couple of miles from Donner Pass—which lies about ten miles west of, and two thousand feet above, Truckee, California."

"So we're in California?"

"That's right. The Golden State," Bandit said. "Though just over the Nevada border."

"So why can't we just walk down to Truckee and telegraph to my father? Ten miles isn't far."

"That's what the Donner Party thought," he said with a grim smile.

"Don't you have a horse?"

"On its first step, the poor thing would be stuck up to its belly until spring. Lou, let me be as clear as I may about your current location. You're in some of the most rugged terrain on the continent, at more than seven thousand feet above sea level. And in minutes the sky can go from clear and blue into a howling blizzard that will make earth and sky look the same. In these parts, ten miles might as well be ten thousand."

She sighed heavily. "And how would I know if you are telling me the truth about all this, or trying to hold me here against my will . . . to satisfy your own inflamed fantasies?"

He sighed back, imitating her. "Believe me, if I could carry you on my back to Truckee right now, I'd do it. And allow me to assure you that any blazing fantasies I might have entertained have long since been snuffed out under an avalanche of cold reality."

Lou folded her arms across her chest. "You must be very proud of yourself, always with some sharp riposte at the ready. Do you think up these things while I'm asleep?"

"*Riposte?*" he laughed. "'Sojourn,' and now 'riposte'? You are truly one of a kind, Lou."

⸺ ∿ ⸺

WHEN DARKNESS AGAIN CAME down—which was early in the high, hidden valley—Bandit lit the candle on the bedside table, another in the far corner of the cabin, and a third next to the stove so that they could read until it was time to turn in.

"What time is it?" Lou asked after the candles had flickered yellowly for an hour or two.

"No idea."

"You don't know what time it is?"

"What difference would it make? I get up with the sun and go to sleep soon after it goes down. Candles are hard to come by, and I have just enough kerosene to run my railroad lantern when I need to. So by my standard, we've already stayed up quite late—at least an inch of candle. *Three* candles. While I'm sure it didn't register, I'm trying to make things feel homey for you."

"You needn't trouble yourself on my account," she said. She looked over at her carpetbag and gave an exaggerated yawn and stretch. "Well, I think I may have just a few little drops of my sleeping draught and retire for the night."

"Getting the itch, are you?"

"I am not getting any *itch*, whatever that means."

"It's what addicts call the craving they get for their drug. The *itch*. The problem with your particular tipple's itch is that it takes ever-increasing quantities to scratch it. But beware . . . because I can tell you for a fact that, at the rate you're going, that little bottle of yours is not going to last the winter."

She had to admit to herself that he was right. The container had been full on the train, but now the magic elixir had begun to creep below the long neck of the glass bottle. And she knew he was also correct that over time she had required more and more to achieve the desired effect. At first, it was only a few drops. Then ten. And twenty. Now she needed a teaspoon at a time—a hundred drops—to reach the thrilling numbness that a tenth of that had given her not so very long ago. And she had already calculated that, even if she *could* somehow limit herself to a teaspoon, in her bottle remained at most fifty more flights of bliss. What then?

"I'm not going to worry about that now," she said.

"Well, bully for you—but I am. Because when you run out, I'm going to have a raving maniac on my hands. In a fifteen by twenty cabin . . . in the deepest reaches of the High Sierra . . . in the dead of winter. Sorry, but I don't welcome that day."

Louisa grunted, retrieved her bottle from her bag, and—without even turning away from him—eased what she gauged was a teaspoonful of the precious fluid into her mouth. She swallowed, wincing. It was impossible to grow accustomed to the piercing bite and acrid bitterness of the stuff, but as soon as its aftertaste began to fade she felt its indescribable warmth oozing like lava from the center of her body. In seconds her feet and fingers and lips had gone beautifully numb and dead.

"*Much* better," she said, and drifted back across the cabin and into bed. She lay motionless on her back, watching the ceiling timbers move and pulse like clouds across a summer sky.

Bandit climbed in next to her and blew out the candle. "Feel good now?"

"I feel absolutely *wonderful*," she said into the fragrant darkness. "But thank you for asking."

"Why do you like it so?"

"Don't get any ideas, mister. There isn't enough for both of us."

"I don't need any bad habits, thank you. I'm simply curious."

"When I'm high, I can forget."

"What are you trying to forget?"

"Everything," she said.

"Lou, I would give everything I have if you would only stop."

"You mean to say that *all this* could be *mine*?" she mumbled, half-asleep.

"All this and more," he said.

AFTER THEIR FIRST TWO somewhat awkward weeks together, Lou and Bandit began to settle into a rhythm. Wake up, have coffee and something to eat, and Bandit would either busy himself with his chores or lash on his snowshoes and go out hunting for game. Even in the dead of winter, the mountains seemed to be full of life. Rabbit and mule deer became regular and, to Lou's changing taste, rather appetizing fare. And there were beans—always beans, taken from the big burlap sacks that Bandit had somehow lugged all the way up the mountain.

As Lou grew accustomed to her new surroundings, and the furor of the big city died away, each item—the coffee pot, the books, Bandit's rifle—became an object of her curiosity. She peppered him with questions about his selection of books, how he had learned to hunt, and a thousand other things.

"You're quite the chatterbox," he said in the middle of one of these interrogations.

"I suppose I'm trying to make sense of all this."

"Then by all means, feel free," he replied. "I will admit it's nice to have someone to talk with."

But there was one subject, only one, that Bandit refused to entertain questions about: the big steamer trunk at the far end of the cabin.

"Bandit," she asked idly one day as he was deep into *King Lear*, "what's in the trunk?"

"What trunk?"

"Oh, you hadn't noticed? There's a gigantic steamer trunk over there."

"That? Nothing."

"It's empty?"

"No, but there's nothing in it that concerns you. You needn't trouble yourself about it."

"Now you're making me curious," she wheedled. "Come on, tell me what's in the trunk!"

He put his Shakespeare down in his lap and fixed her with a stare. "I said, don't trouble yourself about my trunk. It is the only thing in this cabin that's off-limits to you. And that means I don't want you rummaging around in it, or even opening it. Are we clear?"

"Good heavens, you'd think—"

"Are we *clear*?"

"Yes," she said quietly. "We're clear."

He went back to his book, breathing hard.

10

Omnia Vincit Amor

Early December

Lou's second month in the mountains started out clear and bitterly cold. Bandit kept a mercury thermometer nailed to the outer wall of the cabin, sheltered under the eaves from the worst of the weather. One morning, when he came in from emptying the chamber pot and letting Mutt relieve himself, Bandit stamped his feet and hustled over to the woodstove, shivering.

"Good Lord, it's cold today," he said.

"How cold?"

"I don't know. *Cold.*"

"Didn't you look at the thermometer?"

"It's frozen solid."

"It's *frozen*? It's a thermometer. How could that be?"

"The mercury in it. Mercury freezes at just above minus forty. So it's colder than that."

"That's astonishing!"

"Accordingly, I propose we stay inside today," he said, "and keep the fire hot."

"Do we have enough wood?"

He eyed the pile at the end of the cabin. "We should. If not, I'll split some more."

"You seem to enjoy splitting wood."

"I do. It's mentally absorbing and excellent exercise, too."

"Maybe you can show me how to do it sometime?"

"You? Split wood?"

"Why not? Do you think that because I'm a woman, I can't split wood?"

He blinked. "Yes, I suppose that is what I thought."

"I award you partial credit for honesty, but a big fat zero for diplomacy. Stick around, lump. You'll find out that there's a lot you don't know about me yet."

⁓

THE COLD SNAP CLUNG on for more than a week, and then the skies above the High Sierra turned—and stayed—dark and threatening, emitting deep, booming thunderclaps which made the cabin shudder and the plates rattle. And as the days grew ever shorter, when the feeble sun finally succumbed, in minutes night dropped over their cabin like a curtain.

"We should probably begin husbanding our candles," Bandit said one evening as the daylight began to dwindle. "With two of us here now, we're going through them faster than usual. So I'm sorry to say that we'll have to limit our reading after sundown."

"Just when I thought this so-called adventure couldn't get more deadly dull," she groused.

"We'll just go to bed earlier," he said, attempting to cheer her up. "You'll see—it'll be fun."

"No doubt. A real barrel of monkeys."

Lou secretly welcomed the earlier bedtimes, though, if only because they allowed her to take her nightly sleeping draught sooner and sooner. Then she could slide into bed, with Bandit close by, and lose herself until morning. But very recently her nightly dose of laudanum had begun to have a most unpleasant and unexpected effect: Instead of soothing her to sleep, it had begun to make her irritable. Unless she took a little more each night, she would become jittery and sleepless, or find herself plagued by strange and vivid dreams—and if Bandit so much as brushed against her in the night, she'd growl and give him a sharp elbow in the ribs.

TRUE TO BANDIT'S PREDICTION, by mid-December only about half of Lou's bottle of laudanum remained. He had quit pestering her about it, though; he probably knew that her limited supply meant that her quitting the drug was inevitable—only the timing was in doubt.

Lou knew it, too, and if she had misgivings about herself to begin with, she now seriously disliked the person that the delicate opium poppy was turning her into—surly, short-tempered, and lately without any interest in much of anything at all, except whiling away the time until sunset. And her prickly mood was beginning to wear even on the usually affable, imperturbable Bandit.

"Imagine, Lou," he said one night, "in only about two weeks, I'll be wishing you a Merry Christmas. Isn't the time just flying by? Before you know it, you'll be back on the Frisco train."

"Still three or four months to go after Christmas," she said, flopping onto her back. "Might as well be a lifetime."

"Are you really so bored here?"

"Not any more bored than I was in Manhattan, if you want the truth."

"Now *that* is unexpected. How could *Manhattan* be boring?"

She lay there quietly for a moment. "I suppose it's not Manhattan. Or here. I'm bored with *myself*."

"How could that be? You're a young, intelligent—"

"You had better *not* say persnickety."

"I wasn't planning to. My point is that if I find you interesting, why don't you find yourself interesting?"

"You find me interesting?"

"Of course I do. Very interesting."

"Well, I don't. My fiancé made me interesting, but now he's gone."

"Someone else can't make you interesting, Lou."

"Hmm. You know what I'm interested in?"

"No, what?"

"Getting some sleep," she snapped.

———

Two days later, in the wee hours of the morning, Lou awoke shivering and in a cold sweat, although Bandit was still lying snugly against her. She knew immediately what it meant, so she climbed gingerly over his sleeping form and stood quietly by the bed. Then—for the first time ever in the morning—she unstoppered her laudanum bottle and greedily gulped down another teaspoonful.

The drug quickly calmed her; the shivering stopped, and she snuck back into bed next to Bandit, congratulating herself that all her gymnastics had not awakened him.

She had almost fallen into a numb sleep when Bandit abruptly turned to face her. He propped himself up on an elbow, and Lou pretended not to notice.

"Stop faking," he said. "I know you're not asleep."

"I'm not faking anything. I was just now drifting off."

"How about a little story before you do?" he asked.

"Do I have a choice?"

"It's not a long story."

"Praise be," she said.

"Now that's the spirit! All right, here goes. You see, Lou, I have a brother. Actually, I have both a brother and a sister. Both younger than I am. Now, as sometimes happens, my family always had very high expectations for my brother—"

"How surprising! Even after their eldest had made them so proud as a mountain man."

He let her comment pass. "—and sometimes other people's expectations can be a terrible burden."

"You don't say," she said.

"I do say. In time, my brother came to believe he could never live up to my parents' image of him, and he began to dislike himself. He felt he was a failure. And when people start to dislike themselves, they often will do most anything they can to push that thought out of their minds. So he started taking drugs—morphine and chloral and lots of other things, and always more and more of all of them. Yet for all of that, he only liked himself less and less. And he was destroying his health, too."

Lou heaved a deep sigh. "This is, without any doubt, the most depressing story I have ever heard."

"Now hang on a minute, because it has a happy ending. Of course, we all tried what we could to get him to stop. Nothing worked, and we were at wits' end when, quite out of the blue, he met a very special young woman who saw in him things he could not see in himself. They fell in love, and that love restored my brother's will to live."

"And?" she asked, somewhat cautiously.

"He resolved to stop taking the drugs. As you might expect, he went through a week of torment doing it, but his lady was right by his side the whole time. He shook off his addiction, and soon afterward the two of them were married. At the time I left New York, they were expecting their first child."

"That *is* a happy ending," Lou said, sniffling. "Love really did conquer all."

"That it did. My brother found the love of a good woman, of course—but even more important, he learned to love *himself*. And so can you, Lou."

"Ha," she said. "*Love* myself. That's rich. I don't even *like* myself."

"Why not? I like you."

"You do?"

"Sure I do. You must know that."

"I thought I was just a coddled city girl."

"You are, but I like you just the same."

"You're only saying that because you have to spend Christmas with me."

"Not so, but I *am* glad you brought up Christmas. I've been thinking—"

"Don't you ever *stop* thinking?"

He chuckled. "I've been thinking about what I'd like you to give me for Christmas."

"Maybe I could whittle something. Though I wouldn't know what."

"It's not a *what*. It's a *who*. A person I'd like to see again."

"Good luck with that. There's not another human being around for miles."

"Then that will make it easy. Because the person I want to see again . . . is the Lou I saw in the cave, that first day we went outside."

She was quiet for a while. "I told you—that was silly."

"You say that, but I know better. What I saw that day was the *real* you. The wonderful, sensitive woman you try so very, very hard to keep locked away inside."

"Why in the *world* would I do something like that?" Lou said, rolling her eyes.

"Because the *real* you is such a wonderful person that if you looked her straight in the eye, you'd know immediately you were wrong about her. And that you can't abide."

There was another long silence, broken only by Mutt's soft snoring.

"Do you really believe all that, Bandit?" Lou asked, just as Bandit had concluded that she had indeed drifted off.

"Believe all what?"

"That there's a different person—a better person—locked away inside of me?"

"I haven't the slightest doubt of it. You have only to set her free."

"But what if I can't?" she said softly.

"I *know* you can. But first, you have to stop drowning her in laudanum."

Lou was quiet again. "I want to stop, Bandit. I do, but I'm scared I won't succeed. And you said yourself that your brother went through torments."

"He did, but he made it through. You will, too."

"I'm not so sure."

"Then for now, let me be sure *for* you," he said. "I will be here with you the whole time."

Without thinking about it, she snuggled closer to him, feeling his strength.

"Then tomorrow I will begin," she said.

To her shock, he leaned over and kissed her quickly on the forehead.

⁓

By mid-morning, Lou was already restless and irritable, snapping at Bandit over the smallest things: the coffee was too strong, the beans too salty, even how silly her fur-lined trousers looked. He bore it all with good cheer, knowing that the demon inside her had to leave before she could ever be Lou.

The ensuing days, though, were worlds more difficult. Lou took turns sweating, vomiting, and feeling so feeble that Bandit had to help her on and off the chamber pot, which even in her weakened state she found mortifying. All the while, he spoke softly to her in his soothing baritone, never losing his composure, even when he had to clean her backside after problems with the thunder mug.

"I can't do this, Bandit," she said on the third day. "I'm not strong enough."

And he stroked her cheek and said, "You *can* do it, Lou. You're far stronger than you know."

On the fourth day, she begged him either to give her the bottle or put a bullet in her brain. When he refused to do either one, she cursed and spat at him, using every nasty word she could summon to mind, making fun of his beard and his cabin and his stupid, reclusive, monastic life, and just who in the hell did he think he was to tell her what to do with hers?

Yet through it all, Bandit sat with her calmly as she raved, sleepless on the edge of the bed, ferociously loyal, leaving her only briefly to take Mutt outside or to get himself a hunk of salt beef. But then he'd be right back, sitting again and talking to her in that calming voice, reading Shakespeare aloud, telling silly jokes, and even crooning Christmas carols to make her think of the better days ahead and the coming of the Christ child.

At the end of a very, very long week, Lou was drawn, pale, and weak, but *different.* She noticed things about Bandit that she had previously either overlooked or mocked. She paid him compliments on his coffee and his beans, even when they were too salty. And she smiled the pretty smile that she had hidden away for so long that she thought it had been lost forever.

One afternoon, not long after the tempest had passed, Bandit was busily hauling in some wood for the fire, whistling softly to himself as he was wont to do. As he put a few more pieces into the stove to keep her warm, she looked up at him.

"Bandit?" she said.

"Yes, Lou?"

"Thank you," she replied. "From the bottom of my heart. *Thank you.*"

He tried to shrug it off. "Oh, there's nothing to thank *me* for," he said, suddenly hoarse. "You did it all yourself. I'm only sorry you had to suffer so."

She reached up and took his hand, which seemed to flummox him entirely.

"Bandit," she said, trying not to chuckle at his shocked expression, "listen to me. I *didn't* do it all myself. You were with me every painful step of the way. So I am truly grateful—and it would mean a great deal to me if you would accept my thanks."

He blinked, nodded, and cleared his throat. Then he had to turn away.

"You are more than welcome, Lou," he mumbled, patting her hand. "You are indeed."

"That's better," she said.

Bandit still didn't turn around, but instead gently freed his hand from hers. "You know," he said, "I think I'd better split some more wood while the sun's still up." With that he darted back outside, the door closing with a bang in his wake.

Lou waited a moment, and then stood and peered out the window. She liked observing him unawares when he was at his favorite chore, which he accomplished with such practiced skill and gusto that it looked almost like a magic trick. But Bandit was not, as usual, hefting his axe out by the chopping block; instead he was doubled over near it, hugging his knees and sobbing. She thought momentarily to rush out and comfort him, but reconsidered. *He has a right to his own feelings,* she thought, *without mine getting in their way.*

As time passed, Lou didn't remember much about those lost and terrible days spent under the spell of opium, except this: that for too much of her young life she had yearned to die, and that one horrible week had marked an end to all that. Now she wanted only to *live*.

11

Christmas

"Merry Christmas!" Bandit said one bright morning.

"Is it Christmas already?"

"Well, I think so. I may be off by a day or two either way, but we're close. And anyway, if we decide that it's Christmas... then Christmas it is."

"Then a very Merry Christmas to you, too, Bandit! I'm sorry I don't have anything for you under the Christmas tree. If we had a Christmas tree, that is."

"But we do!" he said. "A whole forest of them. And I'll bet you never imagined your Christmas tree would be a hundred feet tall."

"I'm from Manhattan," she said. "Buildings are a hundred feet tall, but certainly not trees."

"What you have been missing," Bandit said. "And I'll tell you another thing: If you ever decide to return to this part of the world, you must see the giant sequoias. They're west of here, almost to the coast. Now *those* are really big trees. They can grow to *three* hundred feet, if you can believe it, and twenty or more wide."

"That's astonishing," Lou said. "They must be very ancient."

"Indeed they are. In fact, some of them are thought to be far older than Christmas itself. Some may be as much as three thousand years old."

"Imagine that . . . they were already a thousand years old on the first Christmas Day."

"It's almost incomprehensible, isn't it? I like to imagine what wisdom such trees must possess."

She laughed. "Trees don't have wisdom, silly."

"Now where's your Christmas spirit? We are surrounded by miracles. It's just that most of the time we overlook them. We think *we're* the miracle."

"There's more truth in that than I care to admit. I wonder what miracles I've overlooked?"

He tapped his lips with a finger. "Well, here's one that I didn't know about until I came out here," he said. "Trees in this very forest, the really old ones, when they are nearing the end of their lives, do you know what they do?"

"I do not."

"A big pine that's close to its natural death—even if it looks perfectly healthy to us—will put out a bumper crop of cones, sometimes so many they pile up almost knee-deep under a hundred-foot-tall tree. The next year or the one after, the tree is dead."

"But how can it know that it's going to die? And why so many pine cones just when it ought to be conserving its strength?"

"I can't answer the first question," he said. "But somehow it does. Now as to your second question, I'll let you think about it for a minute, and it will make perfect sense."

She pondered this for a minute. "I think I understand. It's their last great deed before capitulating. They want to ensure that there will be another generation of trees just like themselves."

His face creased into a big smile. "And you know, I like to think they see death as a triumph, perhaps the greatest act of faith they've ever made in their long lives. Even though they know that they are dying, they believe that death is not the end. Their final act is a celebration of life itself—a gift to the future."

Lou looked away, suddenly conscious of the tears running down her face. "Oh my goodness," she whispered. "It's such a terrible and beautiful thing."

"Well said. And you know, this little tree-miracle is something I always find myself thinking about at Christmas. Christ was born on this day, so long ago, with the knowledge—like those trees—that he must soon die . . . but also knowing that from his death would spring eternal life. Every tree in this forest reminds me of his example."

She stared at him for a moment, tears still trickling over her cheeks.

"My whole life," she said at last, her voice catching, "I've dreamed of *having* things. A fine house, a wealthy husband, why—even an apartment in Paris, of all things. But I had it all backward. What matters is not how much one can *have*—it's how much one can *give*. Right up to the very end—like those lovely, lovely trees." She put her head in her hands and wept, her shoulders heaving in great, wracking sobs, while he sat quietly by, letting her feel.

With some effort, she stopped crying and composed herself. "Oh, how silly and stupid I must look," she said as flatly as she could manage, wiping her eyes with the back of her hand. "I promised I'd never do *that* again, and yet here I am."

"Lou," he said gently, "now *don't*. Do you remember what I asked you for—for Christmas?"

She looked down, biting her lip. "Yes, I remember," she said. "A *who*, not a *what*."

"Well, only a moment ago you gave her to me. So now . . . like any other gift, you can't take her back. Ever."

At that, Lou's eyes welled up again and overflowed, and this time she let them run as freely and unchecked as the little creek outside their cabin door.

She caught her breath and looked into his eyes. "It doesn't seem like enough—"

He reached out and placed his finger softly on her lips. Reflex told her to pull away, but that was replaced by another, softer impulse—the desire to kiss it. She did neither, but simply remained still.

"Shhh," Bandit said. "Not only is it *enough*—it's *everything*. Lou, you've made this the finest Christmas of my life. And in return—while I know it's not the kind of holiday you expected when you left New York—allow me to wish you a very Merry Christmas, my dear."

She thought to remind him that she wasn't his *dear*, but she wasn't so sure anymore.

12

Solomon in All His Glory

January 6, 1900

andit was examining the calendar when Lou opened her eyes and rolled over.

"You certainly do like looking at that calendar," she said.

"Well, today is an important day," he replied.

"How so?"

"By my reckoning, today is Saturday."

"So? Saturday, Sunday, Wednesday . . . they're all the same up here."

"Not in my world, they're not. Saturdays are special."

"I'll bite. Why are Saturdays special?"

"Saturday is bath day."

"You take *baths*? In the *winter*?"

"First of all, thank you very much. And second, yes I do. Although in winter I'll admit it's not every week. It's too much work, because one needs hot water."

"But how does one bathe at all? Without freezing to death, that is."

He pointed to the far end of the cabin. "The washtub over there.

I drag it outside, fill it with water or snow, and build a fire around it. In an hour or two I have a nice, hot bath under the trees and the sky."

"Well, have fun," she said, pulling the blankets over her head. "I'm not doing anything of the sort."

"Oh yes you are."

"Am not."

"Am too. Look, because you've been through so much since you arrived, I haven't mentioned it. But, believe me, you need a bath."

"What kind of crack is that? I use the washbasin twice a day."

"Maybe so, but you stink."

She sat up in bed, her pretty brown waves falling over the puffy shoulders of her nightdress. "I do not *stink*!" she said indignantly.

"You don't think so, because you can't smell yourself. *I* can smell you, though."

"Now you're just being insulting."

"Not really. In the middle of last night, you put your arms over your head and I almost choked to death."

"What a thing to say!"

"You asked me always to tell you the truth. So there it is." He went over to the far end of the cabin and began removing hams and other foodstuffs from the big tub. While his back was turned, Louisa held out the neckline of her nightdress, stuck her face into the opening, and inhaled. *Good God!* she thought in horror. *He's right. I do* stink!

She rearranged her nightdress. "Then if you are going to force me to take a bath, I suppose I'll have to comply."

"A wise decision. For us both."

He dragged the tub to the door, opened it with a practiced foot, and lugged the thing outside. He was gone for a few minutes. When he popped his head back inside, woodsmoke wafted into the cabin.

"I'll have to shovel it full of snow," he said. "The creek's mostly frozen over. You want to go first?"

"I don't know. How long will it take to refresh the bath if you go first and I follow you?"

He looked surprised. "*Refresh the bath*? There's no refreshing the bath. You get in after I get out."

"You mean to say that I'm to plunge myself into your filth?"

"I'm not sure I'd call it *filth*, but yes, that's what I'm saying. It's a lot of work to fill a tub this size and get it hot. I'm not doing it twice in one day!"

"Then I will most definitely go first."

"Fair enough. When you're done, I'll plunge myself into *your* filth."

"Oooh, you!"

He went back outside and this time was gone for the better part of a half hour. She could hear the rhythmic crunch of his shovel blade in the crusty snow and the hollow thud of snow filling up the metal tub.

"Now we have only to wait for it to get hot," he said when he came back inside, huffing and puffing, his face red with cold and exertion.

She sat up in bed while he busied himself with whatever he was always busy with, mending things or carefully cleaning and oiling his rifle. Imagine, she thought, a bath *outdoors*. I've never heard of such a thing.

"Bandit," she said after a while, "may I ask you a question . . . about the bath?"

"Another one?"

"Just one more."

"Let fly, then."

"Won't I catch cold when I get into the bath? Or afterward? It's freezing out there."

"Not if you're quick," Bandit said. "I usually just shuck my duds in here, run out and jump in the tub, relax a bit, and then hurry back in and dry off in here."

Her eyes went wide. "You can't be *serious.*"

"Oh, but I am. If you undressed outside, your clothes would get all cold, and would you really want to pull cold clothing over wet skin? Sometimes you make absolutely no sense at all."

"I'm thinking of my privacy," she said. "I can't have some lonely mountain man ogling me in a state of nature."

"You know," he said, coming over and sitting on the edge of the bed, "this privacy fetish of yours is starting to become quite a nuisance. We have to live together for several more months at least, in a fifteen-by-twenty log cabin. There's no toilet chamber, no changing facilities, and yet you've already adapted to those inconveniences. But your constant insistence on my turning this way or that, or hiding under the covers lest I see a square inch of your flesh, is really getting tedious."

"What other alternative is there, smarty pants? Privacy is privacy, even here. It's not a *fetish.*"

He stood and faced her. "You know what we have to do?"

"What?"

"Get naked."

"I beg your pardon! And just as I was beginning to feel somewhat safe from ravishment."

He looked at the ceiling. "You and your ravishment. As I've told you more times than I can count, I'm *not* going to ravish you, Lou MacGregor. Not for love nor money."

"You don't have to be *quite* so declarative all the time, you know," she said, slightly hurt. "But if you don't have evil designs, why else would you suggest such a thing as . . . why, I can barely say it out loud . . . *getting naked*?"

"Because it's like jumping into cold water. The fear of doing it is so much worse, and so much more prolonged, than plunging right in and getting used to it. So I propose that we both disrobe, even if briefly, and eliminate whatever mystery there is about what's under our duds."

"Ha!" she scoffed. "I'd sooner die."

"Your choice," he said, slipping his suspenders down over his broad shoulders. "But if you're going first in the bath, I'll be stripped down and waiting when you return. So you might as well get a good eyeful now, and we'll never have to have this nonsensical conversation again. In fact, I'm taking it all off right now."

"Don't you *dare*!"

"Sorry, but I've made up my mind at last. It's too darn hot in here for clothes, anyway. As you have experienced firsthand, with the stove roaring this little place gets like a bake-oven."

"This is nothing short of . . . visual ravishment!"

"Then you may shut your virginal eyes. But I'm still taking it all off, regardless. Full steam ahead!"

She turned to face the wall, fuming, but could hear the sound of clothing dropping to the floor and a little cough.

"I'm ready if you'd care to take a gander," Bandit said.

"I will *not* have a gander, or a glimpse, or even a glance. Go away!"

"Where am I supposed to go? We have one room."

"I don't know! Just *go*." She clapped her hands over her eyes and turned her face to the ceiling.

"You know I'm going to stand here until you look," he said. "Somehow we have to get past this weird aversion you have to the human form."

"You can stand there all day if you like."

"Don't you want your morning coffee?"

"What does coffee have to do with anything?"

"Because you like my coffee, and I won't make it for you until you look. So take a peek, and I'll put the pot on. By the time we're done drinking my delicious coffee, your bath will be nice and hot."

"You really won't let me be, will you?" she said, exasperated.

"In a space this small, it's going to happen eventually. So let's get on with it."

"Oh fine!" she said. "I'll look."

She opened her eyes under her hands, and spread her fingers apart just enough to see out. Bandit was indeed standing in the middle of the room, stark naked.

Until now, it had been difficult—impossible, actually—to tell what this man really looked like under his bulky mountain-man garments and the voluminous nightshirt he wore to bed. They made him look shapeless and amorphous, but in the flesh he was anything but. His handsome face was set atop a powerful neck and a set of broad, strong shoulders; below his big chest was a chiseled abdomen that showed every muscle and sinew beneath the skin; and—she summoned her courage to look down—there were his *parts* dangling between two muscular thighs.

Lou wanted to study his penis; she'd never seen one in person before, only in photographs that the girls at school giggled over. But she didn't dare.

He read her mind. "It's just another part of the anatomy," he said, waggling it casually with one hand. "Every male animal has one of some kind or another, so don't make too much of it. Now look at the other side and we're all done." He spun around, and she took her time examining his broad, muscular back and narrow waist and hips. It was a body capable of anything, she found herself thinking, robust and in the prime of life and manhood. She had never beheld anything like it.

"Finished?" he said after a while.

"Quite," she said, somewhat reluctantly. "I've had more than my fill of your peacock display, thank you very much."

"Peacock display!" he said, chuckling. "The things you come up with, Lou."

She watched him dress himself, that perfect body again disappearing under cloth and leather, and didn't bother to turn away.

"Now that wasn't all that bad, was it?" he said when he was again fully clothed. "You noticed no obvious deformities, I trust?"

"Certainly *not*," she said, blushing. "I mean to say, certainly not that it wasn't a terrible thing to have to endure, but no, I didn't detect any obvious deformities."

"And you weren't ravished by your cabinmate, either, were you?"

"I was not, thankfully," she said, though a secret part of her wished he had *tried*, in his usual gentle way. At least it would have been a compliment. She could always have rebuffed him and preserved her honor.

"Thank God *that's* over," Bandit said. "And now I shall make you some coffee."

The coffee was as delicious as ever, and since Lou was feeling that she had just done something a little spicy, it tasted even better.

"I still cannot *believe* that you disrobed right in front of me," she said into her mug. "You are, without exception, the most shameless man I have ever met."

He shrugged. "Ashamed? On the contrary—I feel liberated. Before you arrived, all I generally wore indoors was moccasins or socks. Period. And now at last I can return to my old ways."

"You will *not* be waltzing around here in the buff," she said.

"Why not?"

Lou found to her surprise that she couldn't muster up a good riposte.

AFTER THEY HAD FINISHED their coffee and a little ham, he poked his head out of the cabin door. As he had predicted, Lou's bath was steaming in the frigid air.

"Your bath is prepared, *mademoiselle*," he said. "Get a move on, now, so that I'll still have some warm water after you're done."

"Look away, then."

"Oh Lord, you're still on *that*," he groaned. "After my peacock display?"

"That was your decision, not mine. Go on now, turn around."

He sighed and turned his chair around. Lou slipped out of her nightdress and gingerly tiptoed out of the cabin. Outside, her bare skin crackled with the cold, and hurriedly she put a foot into the hot water, but it was almost scalding—much too hot for a bath. And there she was, naked in the snow. How could she go back into the cabin, where Bandit might well be watching lasciviously?

She tiptoed back across the crust of snow and rapped gently on the door.

"Who's there?" Bandit's voice said.

"It's m-m-me," she replied, shivering.

"Who?"

"Stop. I'm n-naked out here, and the water's too hot. I n-n-need to come in again and let it c-c-cool off a bit. Turn away!"

He gave a sigh audible through the door, which then creaked open. She retrieved her nightdress and hurriedly slipped it over her head.

"Satisfied?" he said.

"For now, yes. I'll go back out in just a few minutes."

"God, you defy description," he mumbled. "Next time, I'm going first, whether you like it or not."

They waited for a few minutes. "All right, mountain man," she said. "You know the drill. Turn!" She spun her index finger around in midair.

He repeated the process, and out she tiptoed again. The water was still quite hot, but she eased herself down inch by inch, and soon enough she found it tolerable. She leaned her head against the back of the tub and looked up through the snowy ponderosa pines to a brilliant cerulean sky. The vapor of her breath mingled with the cloud of steam curling up from the tub.

Magical, she thought. Just magical.

She ran her hands over her body, and her skin felt alive—alive in a way it had never felt before, racing with blood and with the whole idea of being exposed in the greatness of Creation. Then her city mind took over again.

Soap! There's no soap!

"Bandit!" she yelled.

The cabin door opened, and she slid down below the waterline.

"Are you all right?"

"I forgot the soap. Would you get it for me?"

"Back in two shakes," he said, and banged back into the cabin. He returned with a big hunk of yellow soap in his hands.

"Toss it over!"

He rolled his eyes and lobbed the soap over to her. She put up her hands to catch it, and briefly the top part of her torso came out of the water.

"Ha!" Bandit exulted. "I just saw your titties!"

She scowled. "You are no gentleman! And you did not see my . . . whatever you called them."

"*Titties,*" he snickered, puffing out steam.

"That is simply crude. And you did not see them."

"I don't know what the problem is," he said. "They were very shapely titties, and the right one has a most charming little birthmark. I found them both to be quite fetching."

"Go back into your lair, ogre!" she howled. "I've had quite enough of this."

He laughed. "Now don't hog all the hot water. Get nice and clean and let me have a turn."

She waved the back of her hand at him. "Go away, you big lump."

He went back into the cabin, and she lay back again, rubbing the soap under her arms and then between her legs, which tingled oddly—something she hadn't quite felt before, or at least not in this way and in such circumstances.

Silly fool, she thought. *Only a few months ago, you were engaged to the scion of one of the finest families of New York, and now you're sitting in a washtub in the middle of nowhere, thinking naughty thoughts about a* mountain man? Though, she reassured herself, he *is* an unusually good-looking mountain man.

Lou lingered for a few more minutes, and either she was becoming accustomed to its heat, or the bathwater was starting to cool, so she thought it would only be fair to let Bandit have his turn.

She got out, rapped softly on the cabin door, and when she heard nothing from within, slipped inside. Bandit was reading by the stove, dutifully turned toward the wall. There was a large, clean towel folded by the door. Lou picked it up, dried herself off, and fastened it above her breasts.

"Enjoy your bath?" he asked the wall.

"It was very pleasant," she replied to the back of his head. "I have only to get dressed, and it's all yours."

"Just let me know when you're ready."

She padded over to the bed, where her fur-lined trousers and denim shirt were lying. She picked up the shirt and was about to slip her arms into it when she had another thought. *Maybe he's right about this, too. Maybe I am being silly, or naughty, or both—but then again, I haven't exactly been rewarded for being good or sensible, either.*

"Bandit," she said softly.

"What is it *now*? May I turn around *yet*?"

"You may."

He turned, and his normally placid expression was replaced by one of shock. Lou was standing by their bed, entirely in the nude, looking him directly in the eye.

"What in the *devil*—"

She held her arms out at her sides. "I hope it's not *too* devilish," she said with a little grin. "But I felt like such a sybarite in that lovely bath that I began to think that you may be right after all. This privacy stuff is fine for the city, but not so much in the wilderness. So here I am. Take a good look and we'll call it even."

Her body was magnificent. A graceful neck, firm breasts, a narrow waist that needed no corset, and long, supple legs that, at their apex, terminated in a neat little patch of hair. There was a short purplish scar on the lower right-hand side of her abdomen. She twirled around, as though modeling a new outfit, looking at him coyly over her shoulder.

Bandit was thunderstruck by this spectacle, this goddess. Lou turned and faced him again, this time putting her hands on her hips and looking him directly in the eyes. The blood was pounding hard in her temples, and she found this exhibition—this unabashed, forthright display of her womanhood—powerfully arousing.

"*Well?*" she said.

"Well what?" he stammered.

"Well, what do you think?"

"I think . . . I think you're beautiful."

"Then as you bask in my beauty, you may like to know a few things about me. I'm twenty-five years old, and will be twenty-six in June. I have never been married, though as you know I came close once. I am five feet, five and one-half inches tall, and I weigh one hundred and twenty pounds, just as you guessed. I currently retain all of my natural teeth. And I have never been naked in front of any man before this, except of course for the family doctor. Oh, and since we're on the topic"—she traced the angled scar on her abdomen with the backs of her fingers—"this is a souvenir of my appendectomy three years ago, which started all of the trouble you helped me out of."

"I . . . I'm at a loss for words," he said, staring.

"You don't seem to be at a loss for looking."

He snapped his head to the side. "Oh, sorry."

He heard her laugh. "It's fine. Go ahead."

Bandit turned back to look at her again and watched as she pulled on her clothing.

"You *were* right, Bandit. It was silly of me, and I feel much better now. We're just people, after all, no different from the deer and the bears and . . . well, whatever it is you have out here."

"That is wisdom worthy of Solomon," he said, watching her finish dressing and finding himself wishing she would stay unclothed. "There's less difference than we might care to admit between us and the rest of the animal kingdom. And as the Good Book says, look how marvelously they are clothed."

"We'll have a dinner conversation tonight over that, I expect," Lou said, pouring herself a second mug of coffee from the pot piping on the stove. "Now shoo! And get your bath before it freezes over."

Bandit jumped up from his chair and threw off his clothes while Louisa sipped her coffee and approvingly watched his whole striptease.

Then he fairly bounded out of the cabin—either eager for his bath, or unaccountably happy.

When the door closed behind him, she marveled at what she had just done, only six weeks after falling into a numb sleep in a palace car and waking to find herself abandoned and alone. *Six weeks*, she thought to herself. *Is that all?* She found herself smiling, feeling for perhaps the first time in her life that she was comfortable in her own skin. And she could no longer deny that the *old* Louisa MacGregor had been a nice enough person, to be sure—of good stock, a dutiful daughter—but also closed off, afraid to live, and so *coddled* that she had started to become, well—*persnickety*. She looked down at her denim and deerskin and exulted.

She liked the way it felt to be *Lou*.

13

❧

On the Lam

Samuel Proctor and Jack Remington—that's what it said on their WANTED posters, anyway—had been holing up in Truckee after a late-autumn bank heist just across the Nevada line. The pair rightly thought that neither the cops nor the army could follow them across state lines, and so when they made it to Truckee, flush with their stolen cash, they looked forward to a long winter of cards, drinking, and carousing with the professional ladies in the great state of California.

They hadn't reckoned on the Pinkerton Detective Agency, however. The Free Silver Bank, whose name the two had laughed about long after it had ceased to be funny, had not taken kindly to its deposits being stolen, especially not by a pair of small-timers who thought that scurrying across the border would guarantee them immunity. So the bank had hired the dreaded Pinkertons, who didn't forgive and wouldn't forget. The Pinkertons' logo said it all: a single, all-seeing eye that—like the eye of God Himself—could never be hidden from forever.

So damned if Proctor and Remington weren't upstairs in one of their favorite brothels, getting better acquainted with a couple of hired girls, when two of the Pinkertons' meanest agents showed up downstairs. Fortunately, for almost the first time in a lifetime of never thinking more than five minutes ahead, Proctor and Remington had taken care to bribe the bouncer to give them the high sign if anyone suspicious showed up. And so they had fled, on foot and without most of their gear, into the forbidding mountains above Truckee.

Long before the two friends had learned that crime paid better than prospecting, fur trapping, or guiding vacationing city slickers up into the scenic peaks, both had been among the crews that built the stretch of the Sierra Pacific Railroad through the Donner Pass. It had been a few years, but wild country, if left alone, changes only slowly, and they had known it well. So they figured they could do a pretty fair job of losing the Pinkertons in the wilderness without losing themselves in the bargain.

While they had been reveling down in Truckee, it had been impossible not to hear all about the train that had been cut in two, its back half left behind during the first great blizzard of the season. Now on the lam again and with no option except to hide out until spring to make good their escape, Jack and Sam decided to follow the railroad tracks some two thousand feet straight up into the deepest heart of the Sierras, where they knew that even the most dogged Pinkerton would not dare follow.

They fashioned snowshoes out of flexible saplings and strips of bark and twine, and one slow step at a time chased the Sierra Pacific's steel into the sky. They knew that eventually they must come to the stranded train, which would afford both shelter and—most likely— plenty of grub to keep them alive until the thaw. And in a certain style, too—if not quite the Truckee high life, even an abandoned train was far more comfortable than sleeping rough, which in the dead of winter wasn't a realistic option.

The eight-mile hike took two punishing days and nights, and by the time the two reached the snow-covered train, they were both cold, wet, and exhausted. They quickly decided that the three empty passenger cars were of no use to them after all, since the seats were too small to allow enough room to lie down, and their coal stoves wouldn't work without coal. They didn't know that less than ten paces away, hidden beneath the deep drifts, lay more than a winter's worth of the black gold.

The baggage car, though, held more promise. It was locked up tight, but Proctor and Remington knew a thing or two about breaking and entering, so that was no great obstacle. Inside, they found a trove of hams, some rice, and plenty of other foodstuffs destined for the markets of San Francisco. Here, they decided, they would make their winter camp, surrounded by trunks and crates and bags containing who-knew-how-many valuables. They had until spring to feast and to pilfer at their leisure; the pair congratulated themselves that when the thaw came, they would be all the fatter and richer for having been chased out of Truckee by the private dicks.

And, at least for now, they didn't even have to be concerned about the depredations of bears, which, when they awakened from their winter sleep, would be hungry and curious. To bears, humans meant that food must be close by, and a winter-starved bear would gladly kill anything standing between it and its first decent meal of the season. But that was still months away, and Remington and Proctor planned to be long gone by then.

They were surprised to see, sitting just behind the baggage car, a private car—one of the fancy palace cars, to boot. That meant someone with serious money had been on the train, and for a few minutes, Jack and Sam thought they had hit the mother lode. The car was locked up tight, though, and not with the usual padlocks they were used to breaking. They peered through the windows, but while the car was chock-full of fine furnishings, there wasn't any luggage visible. They reasoned that whoever could afford such a car would surely have been permitted to go on to Frisco in possession of his valuables. Thus the effort of forcing entry into a palace car, only to have a look around such an unusual item, seemed too much like hard work. Jack and Sam accordingly scuttled the idea.

That night, the two cooked up some ham and beans. Their campfire had to be kindled outside, of course; there was no safe way to have open flames inside a wooden railroad car. They found a case of whiskey in the baggage car, and so two hours later—drunk as lords and full of ham, beans, and anticipation of a comfortable night's slumber, they spread out their bedrolls on the wooden floor of the baggage car and were soon fast asleep.

But without a fire to keep them warm, by sunrise the two were half-dead of cold. They staggered out of their shelter and resurrected their campfire.

"That's the coldest I've been in as long as I can remember," Proctor mumbled into his muffler, huddling so close to the flames that steam began to rise from his heavy coat. "You know we won't last a week like this, Jack."

Remington mulled this over. "I suppose we can try having a fire inside the damn car. It's a risk, though."

"At this point, I think I'd rather burn up than freeze to death," Proctor said.

So that night, they kindled their fire on a piece of sheet metal inside the baggage car, polished off an entire bottle of whiskey, and hoped for the best. But in short order they discovered that—with the doors and windows all shut tight against the penetrating cold—their baggage car was worse than a smokehouse. They snuffed out the fire in disgust and stood outside in the killing cold, hopping stiffly from foot to foot until the smoke cleared.

Come morning, Remington winced as he peeled off his boots and socks by the campfire. *"Damn,"* he murmured, examining his feet. Several of his toes had turned an unhealthy shade of purplish-black.

"That don't look too good," Proctor said.

"No shit."

Proctor lit his pipe and puffed for a minute or two. "I know this sounds plumb crazy, but I been thinkin' . . . maybe we go back down to Truckee and turn ourselves in. At least jail would be warm."

"It ain't *that* crazy," Remington replied. "I don't much like the idea of another stretch, but . . . what do you think they'd give us? Five years?"

Proctor shrugged. "Who knows? But I'd say at least five. We whacked a hornet's nest this time."

"Shit."

"No good option, pal."

"Then we might as well get going," Remington said, gingerly pulling on his socks and boots.

"Can you make it on them hooves of yours?"

"Don't have much choice, do I?" he said, standing and kicking out their campfire in a shower of sparks.

Proctor hoisted his pack, and together the two began walking slowly back down the rail line. After perhaps two hundred yards, though, Remington stopped abruptly and sniffed the air.

"You smell that?" he asked.

"Smell what?"

"Smoke."

Proctor tested the air. "Our campfire?"

"Huh-uh. That smelled like varnish. This is different. It's woodsmoke."

Proctor scented the air again. "You know, I think you may be right."

Remington looked around, still sniffing. "Well, it sure as hell ain't fire season."

"Say, take a look at that, will you?" Proctor said, pointing over the tops of the lodgepoles, where there was a little plume of greyish smoke rising.

"Well, now how about that. How far away you reckon that is?"

Proctor watched the smoke. "An hour or two, give or take."

"Worth a try. Better to waste a couple hours than five years in jail."

They set off uphill, Remington limping along behind his friend. They chased the scent of smoke for at least two hours, but in the shifting winds of the High Sierra, it seemed to drift toward them from several directions at once.

"I'd bet my life that there's something up here," Remington said, leaning heavily against a tree. "And I aim to find it. But I can't walk no more today."

They turned and retraced their steps downhill. It would mean another freezing night in the baggage car—but they were still alive, if barely.

14

Wolves

As Proctor and Remington were heading back to their baggage car, Lou and Bandit were enjoying a delicious supper of venison and fried bread, though, as usual, doing far more talking than eating.

Bandit would typically raise some topic, from Shakespeare to the Spanish War, which they would then discuss and sometimes debate. In these candlelight contests, the mountain man and the city girl were usually evenly matched, though neither felt any particular need to *win*. So they both simply enjoyed their little game until, all too soon, it was again time to turn in.

Later, as Lou was almost asleep—though finding herself entertaining a few stray thoughts about the beautiful naked body next to her, now dressed neatly in his nightshirt—Bandit gave her a soft nudge.

"Huh?" she blurted out, afraid he had been reading her mind again. "Is something the matter?"

"No. Listen."

They were quiet, and soon enough she heard a peculiar sound—a long, mournful cry, punctuated by sharp yipping. In the moonlight she could make out Mutt's silhouette. He was standing at attention by the door, hackles raised.

"What's that?"

"*Wolves*," Bandit said. "I wanted you to hear them. It's a beautiful sound."

She shrank against him. "I think it's terrifying. They sound like demons."

"If they are demons, they're the most honorable ones you'll meet. They have large and happy families, are loyal partners, and know how to work together as a team. I admire them."

"I don't think you'd find them so admirable if you were out there with them."

"I'd have to play by their rules, that's all."

"Would they be so accommodating if they ever got in here, I wonder?"

He laughed lightly. "You've got me there, Lou. Would you like to put your head on my shoulder?" he asked, quite out of the blue.

"You won't take advantage?"

"You mean ravishment?"

"Any kind of advantage, up to and including actual ravishment."

"I promise I'll be good," he said, and Lou pillowed her head on his shoulder. He pulled her closer to him, and she didn't resist.

"Sleep well, Bandit."

"Sweet dreams, Lou," he replied.

"You know, tonight I think I'll pretend we're a couple of wolves," she murmured, "curled up together under the moon."

He gave her a little squeeze in reply. She snuggled still closer to him and fell asleep to the distant howling of the wolves.

15

Hospitality

By dawn, when the wolves had returned to their dens, Proctor and Remington were just emerging from theirs—the ice-cold baggage car. When their campfire got going, they thawed out a hunk of ham and waited to see if smoke would again rise over the treetops.

And soon enough it did, but plainer this time, since the wind had died away sometime in the night and the air was clear and still.

"Today just might be our lucky day," Proctor said, nodding at the wafting smoke.

Remington scowled. "It better be, or you'll be going to jail by yourself."

The two lashed on their snowshoes and hiked up the slope and into the trees. This time, without the fickle wind to confuse them, they could easily follow the scent, and after an hour or so it was strong enough that they knew they were getting close.

When they came over the top of the ridge, they saw below a long, narrow valley, deep in snow but quite level, and cutting through it a bright little stream. And not twenty yards from the stream sat a tidy little cabin, with the sought-after plume of smoke rising from its chimney.

"Now will you look at *that*?" Proctor said, breaking into a craggy smile. "What did I tell you?"

Remington showed off a mouthful of stained teeth in return. "Sam, I feel like I've died and gone to heaven."

ALTHOUGH IT WAS PAST time to get up, Lou was looking for any excuse to stay in bed, and since Bandit was still snoozing next to her, she didn't need to look far. Normally by this time he would be walking around attending to some little chore, wearing only his socks. In recent days, he'd reverted to his old ways of mostly going about in the buff. Lou didn't even make a show of looking away.

In fact, she liked looking at him, and sometimes—when he wouldn't notice—she stared at him with what she chided herself, if mildly, was nothing short of naked lust. On more and more nights, he chose to sleep in the nude, too, and soon enough she had started joining him, if only to feel the inimitable comfort of skin on skin. And—when she was honest with herself—in case he might have one of those *ideas* she kept thinking about.

But to her growing bewilderment, Bandit remained a perfect gentleman. That said, when he finally stirred and stretched on the morning after they'd fallen asleep to the cries of wolves, she rolled toward him, hoping to put her head on his shoulder to keep him near for a few last precious minutes—and to her surprise bumped into a very full erection poking through his nightshirt.

"Sorry," he said sheepishly, embarrassed for the first time she could recall. "I have to relieve myself, but I was so enjoying lying here with you, I didn't want to get up. Now I'm about to burst."

She found this curious. "You mean it can get like *that* from having to use the toilet?"

He seemed relieved. "Oh yes, frequently that's all it is, in fact." He threw his legs over the edge of the bed and bent over to retrieve the chamber pot. Then he stood, pulling his nightshirt tightly about him.

"Oh, will you look at who's caught the privacy fetish now?" she said. "Don't bother. Come on—let me see it!"

"Nothing doing!"

"I've seen it before," she said, affecting nonchalance. "Lots of times."

"Not like—*this*, you haven't."

"Oh, *please*. Quit stalling, you prude—raise the curtain and let me have a good look at it. Chop chop, now."

He rolled his eyes and pulled his nightshirt up above his waist. She crawled to the edge of the bed and eyed his penis for a few long heartbeats.

"My, my," she said quietly. "That is certainly *nothing* to be embarrassed about. Quite the contrary."

"Very funny," he said. He picked up the chamber pot and was turning to go when she grabbed him by the arm.

"Bandit," she said, "before you go, would you mind if I touched it?"

"Touched it?"

"Yes. I've never touched a man's . . . *thing* . . . before. And especially not in such an *unusual* state."

"Er, I suppose," he said, turning back to the bed and again pulling up his nightshirt. She sat up and tentatively reached out a finger. She tugged down on it and let it spring back up again.

"*Fascinating*," she said, almost to herself. "Truly it is. It reminds me of gutta-percha."

"I'm not quite sure how to take that. And as much as I appreciate your interest, now I really *do* have to go."

Lou followed his firm buttocks as he went to the other side of the room and continued to watch as he held the pot up and urinated into it. There was something about the whole thing that made her ache.

He quickly dumped the pot in the snow outside, and when he returned to bed his penis had mostly relaxed again.

Bandit lay back down next to Lou. "Well, now *that* was a first," he said.

"Thanks for letting me touch it."

"You're more than welcome. I suppose."

"Would you mind if I asked you a question? About *it*?"

"You're twenty-five years old, Lou. Why so much curiosity?"

"Because I haven't had any experience with such—*things.*" She giggled.

"Fine then. Ask away."

"Have you ever . . . you know . . . ?"

"Know what? I haven't the faintest idea of what you're driving at."

"*Used* it?"

"Huh? I just used it a few seconds ago. Unless I'm mistaken, you were watching the whole time, too."

"Not for *that*. I mean . . . well, here goes. Bandit, have you ever engaged in *sexual intercourse*?"

Bandit looked over at her. "For such a prim young lady from a good family, you can be rather forward when you want to be. First gutta-percha, and now this."

"We're trapped here for months, and there's precious little to occupy ourselves other than conversation. You said it yourself."

"Hmm. Well, then—yes, I have engaged in sexual intercourse."

She blinked, feeling her heart rise into her throat. "I *see*. Once, or more than once?"

"For the love of God, Lou."

"Come on now. In for a penny, in for a pound. Once, or more than once?"

"More than once."

"Will wonders never cease," she said with a kind of awe. "How *many* times, would you say?"

"Lou."

"Last question, I promise. Come on—surely you must know how many times you've done such a memorable thing as that!"

He looked up at the ceiling, seeming to calculate something.

"Give or take . . . perhaps three hundred times?" he mused.

She propped herself up on one elbow and gawked at him. "Did you say *three hundred* instances of coition?"

"It's an estimate."

"My word, you *are* an inveterate ravisher, after all."

"I am nothing of the sort." He paused and took a deep breath. "Lou, I was married for two years. So naturally during that time my wife and I had regular sexual relations."

"You were *married*?"

"I was. For two years. Is there an echo in here?"

"I'm merely surprised."

"Why? Don't you think a woman would have me?"

"I don't think that at all. It's just . . . I didn't know."

"You never asked."

"*Three hundred times in two years*," she said quietly. "Amazing."

"It's not so amazing, you stuffed shirt. First of all, it can be quite a lot of fun, if you want to know. And when you love someone, there's something else about it that is very meaningful."

"How so?"

"There's no way you can be closer to someone else. And if you love that person, really love him or her, when you are together in that way, it can feel almost as if your two spirits are joined together."

She fell back onto her pillow. "It sounds rather beautiful when you say it like that—'spirits joined together.' I've only seen photographs of the act, and those seemed . . . well, *naughty*."

He nodded. "The photographs do tend to make it seem naughty. But it's not at all—when love and marriage are involved. That's why you've never been in any danger of being ravished, as you like to say."

"But surely you're not still . . ."

"Married? No. My wife died three years ago, just before I came up here."

"Oh my, Bandit. I *am* sorry. Truly."

"Thank you. So am I."

She was quiet for a long time. "Is that why you came up here? Because you lost your wife?"

"I—"

At that moment there was a loud banging on the cabin door. Bandit leaped out of bed and hurriedly pulled on his clothes. He put his finger to his lips.

"Who is it?" she whispered.

"I don't know, but it's very unusual. Just keep your wits about you."

Bandit opened the door a crack, and a gust of frigid air and snow-flakes forced itself in.

"Help you?" he said to someone.

"Mister, we need a place to bunk for a couple nights," a gruff voice replied. "Our cabin collapsed last night."

"You're lucky to be alive," Bandit said. "Give us just a minute—my wife needs to dress."

"Tell her to hurry up," the voice said. "It's cold as hell out here, and my friend's feet are frostbit."

"Bandit," she whispered when he had shut the door, "I don't like—"

He held up his hand to silence her. "*No time*," he said under his breath.

Lou dressed quickly, and Bandit opened the cabin door again. In stepped two weather-beaten men wearing furs and smoked spectacles. One had a frazzled grey beard stained yellow on either side of his mouth with tobacco juice.

"I'm sorry for your misfortune, boys," Bandit said. "You're welcome to our floor."

"Much obliged," the bearded man said. He spied Lou standing by the bed. "Beg your pardon, ma'am," he said, lifting his hat and sending a cascade of snow onto their clean floorboards.

Lou managed a thin smile in return, and Mutt emerged from under the bed. He began to growl at the two new arrivals.

"Easy, Mutt," Bandit said, and Mutt stopped growling. He lay down in front of Lou, still looking with suspicion on the two visitors.

"That's a damn big dog," the bearded man said, looking sidelong at his companion.

"He can be mean," Lou said, patting Mutt's big head.

"I don't doubt it," the man said, turning back to Bandit. "Name's Sam Proctor. This here's my partner Jack Remington."

"Robin Littlejohn," Bandit said, shaking the men's hands. "You've already met my wife Louisa."

"Pleasure to know you," Proctor said, dropping his fur cape and pack with a heavy thump and a splash of mud and snow. "*Damn*, it's cold out there."

"You'll thaw out quickly now," Bandit said. "Warm yourselves by the stove, why don't you?"

Remington limped over to the woodstove and sat down heavily on the floor, where he began tugging on his boots.

"May I offer you some coffee?" Lou asked, trying to be as hospitable as possible through gritted teeth.

"Long as it's hot," Remington said, and Lou took down the coffee pot from its little shelf near the stove.

"It's a lucky thing you found us," Bandit said. "I don't expect you would have lasted much longer out there."

"No foolin'," Proctor said. "We was about to take our chances and hike down to Truckee, but then my friend's feet went bad. When we saw your smoke, I knew it was a sign from God, and nothing less."

"What is it that brings you up to the high country this time of year, anyway? Hunting or prospecting?"

Remington gave him an odd look over his shoulder. "Little of both, I guess."

"Well, there are some good places around here. Where did you say your cabin was?"

"We didn't," Remington replied, looking away and massaging his swollen feet. "But since you asked, it was east of here. Northeast."

Bandit frowned. "Northeast? There's a big drop-off not far from here in that direction. I wouldn't have thought there'd be any suitable place for a camp over that way."

"Aw, don't pay Jack any mind," Proctor said. "He don't know east from west. Hell, most of the time he don't know his asshole from a hole in the ground."

Bandit frowned. "Now Mr. Proctor—"

Remington sneered. "Least I ain't one."

"Ain't one what?" Proctor shot back.

"An asshole."

"Feet or no feet, I'll knock the livin'—"

"Now what do you know—we're fresh out of water!" Lou said from the stove. "Robin, would you mind helping me fetch some from the creek?"

"Of course, dear," Bandit said.

Proctor emitted a sniffling little laugh. "Damn, Mr. Littlejohn, you are some kind of prince. If my old lady asked me to help her fetch a bucket of water, I'd smack her into next week."

"Mrs. Proctor is a very lucky woman," Lou said under her breath as she took the bucket down from its peg.

Lou and Bandit walked down to the creek, where they knelt to fill the bucket.

"These men have to go," Lou said out of the corner of her mouth. "I don't like them."

Bandit breathed out a great cloud of steam. "Oh, believe me, I don't like them, either. Not even a little. But I can't very well just throw them out."

"Why not? It's our—your—cabin."

"I know, but as I've told you, it's the *code* up here. Anyone who asks for help must be given it. Not forever, but for a few days. It can mean the difference between life and death."

"I don't care about any stupid code. I know unsavory men when I see them."

"You thought *I* was unsavory."

"Shut up. You're a garden-variety ogre with a dirty mind. My father is a judge, and I've seen men like this come before his court. They have a *look* about them."

"Believe me, every prospector has that look," Bandit said.

"They're a bunch of misfits. And most of them are running away from something."

"How long does it take to get a damn bucket of water?" shouted a voice from behind them.

"Had to chip away some ice to get to it!" Bandit shouted back over his shoulder.

"See what I told you?" Lou hissed. "I want them *gone*!"

"And gone they will be—in two days or less," he said. "Try to be patient."

They finished filling the bucket and walked back to the cabin, where Jack Remington was waiting for them, leaning against the doorframe.

16

Divide and Conquer

The day crept slowly by, spent in awkward and, Lou thought, painfully stupid conversation with the two scruffy interlopers. Worse, their story seemed to change a little each time it was told. At first, the cabin had collapsed on them. Then the roof had partially caved in, and they thought it *might* give out. Then it was a window that blew out in a squall.

Bandit fixed the four of them a little supper, which the men ate with what Lou thought had to be even worse table manners than the wolves they'd heard the night before. Remington and Proctor could not have missed the withering stare of disgust she trained on them, but they either didn't let on or didn't care. The meal finished with a steaming mug of the precious Delmonico's coffee.

At long last, the tired sun started to go down, but Lou refused to light a candle. "We turn in early here," she said. "We can't afford to waste candles, even when we have guests."

"Then I reckon it's bedtime," Proctor said.

"I reckon you're right," Lou replied.

In the fading light, the two unfurled their bedrolls on top of the Oriental carpet, stripped to their long johns, and lit their pipes. Bandit laced up his boots, threw his buffalo robe over his shoulders, and took his rifle down from above the door.

"Now where you off to, big man?" Remington asked. "You sure ain't goin' hunting this time of night."

"I have to take my dog out before bed, and"—he held up the rifle—"I'm sure you've heard the wolves lately." He clucked to Mutt, and the dog ran over to the door.

Remington gave Proctor an odd look, and Bandit and Mutt went out into the snow. As soon as the cabin door closed behind them, Remington hobbled over to it and dropped its locking bar into its heavy iron brackets.

"What in the world do you think you're doing?" Lou said.

"What does it look like he's doin'?" Proctor said. "He's makin' sure we got us some privacy."

"That's not funny in the slightest," she said.

"Maybe that's because he ain't joking," Remington said.

"You unlock that door right now! My . . . Mr. Littlejohn will die of cold out there!"

Proctor and Remington laughed. "She catches on pretty durn fast, now don't she, Jack?"

"For a woman," Remington said.

The door rattled against the bar. Bandit's muffled voice came through the thick wood.

"Hey! The door's locked! Open up in there!"

"Let him *in*!" Lou pleaded.

"Lou!" came Bandit's voice. "Lou!"

She was about to yell back to him when Jack Remington pulled a big Colt six-gun from his rucksack. "Make another sound, lady, and I promise I'll drill you right between the eyes."

The door began thudding hard now, as Bandit hurled his big frame against it. But he had built it too sturdy, and the door did not yield. Mutt could be heard snarling and barking.

"Look," Lou said, her eyes wide, "*please* don't let him die out there. You can have anything you want, but you have to open that door!"

Proctor took a match safe from his long johns and lit the candle. His eyes glittered amber in the yellow flame.

"What if it's *you* we want?" he said. "A man does get mighty lonely up in these mountains."

She held out her hands. "Fine. You can do anything you want with me, and I won't stop you. But for God's sake, don't let him die out there."

"Well, I *am* sorry about that," Proctor said, "but it jus' don't work that way. Them two out there are mad as wet hens right about now, and—well, let's say we'd best let 'em cool off."

He fished a fifty-cent piece from his trousers. "Awright . . . what's it to be, Jack? Heads or tails?" he said, flipping the coin into the air.

"Tails," Remington said, as the thudding on the door resumed with what sounded like rising desperation. The coin landed with a soft clatter on the boards, and Proctor bent over to examine it.

"Damn, Jack, tails it is," Proctor said. "I guess tonight I'll take seconds."

"I'll make sure to leave you some," Remington said. "*Strip*," he said to Lou, pointing with his six-shooter.

The thudding on the door had now been replaced with silence, and Lou was nearing panic. She wished that Bandit were here to fight these terrible men—but in a flash she remembered something he had said on that first day they had ventured out into the Sierras: "*One of these days, you may have to fend for yourself—and I want to make sure that I teach you how, should that time ever come . . .*"

That time has come, Lou thought.

"You know, fellows," she said to Proctor and Remington, her tone suddenly light and flirtatious, "I think we may have gotten off on the wrong foot."

Proctor and Remington looked at each other for a long moment.

"What's that supposed to mean?" Proctor said.

"What I mean is that . . . every man worth his salt likes a good stiff drink before he gets a piece."

"You hear that, Jack?" Proctor said. "This lady ain't no shrinkin' violent!"

"You're damn right I ain't," Lou said, trying her best to imitate her captors' drawl. "So before we git down to business, maybe you boys would like some whiskey?"

Proctor grinned. "You know—"

"Come on, Sam," Remington whined. "I'm hard as a railroad spike over here."

"Jack, don't always be in such an all-fired hurry about everything. Ain't nothin' wrong with wettin' our whistle before we wet—"

"Then why don't you two make yourselves comfortable while I fix you a nice whiskey?" she said.

The pair plopped down on the Oriental carpet. "Not there," Lou said, "I won't have you boys sitting on a cold, hard floor. Come over here and sit by me, near the stove."

"Damn, she's right horsepitable, ain't she? Once she's out of options," Proctor said.

Remington burst into mad laughter while Lou knelt to feel for her bottle under the nightstand. After Christmas, she and Bandit had agreed to keep it there, as a reminder of the demon she had conquered.

Lou popped back up, and in the dim light gave the men a winsome look while sending almost all of the remaining laudanum gurgling into two mugs.

"That ought ter do the trick right nice," she said, handing a mug to each of them.

Proctor peered into the liquid and gave it a deep sniff. "This don't smell like any damn whiskey I ever had."

"It's from New York," she said. "Whiskey's different back East."

Remington shrugged, took a big gulp from his mug, and winced. "Damn, lady, if this ain't the bitterest shit I ever tasted, I don't know what is."

"You ain't foolin'," Proctor agreed, swallowing with a grimace. "It's like an unripe persimmon."

"*Persimmon*? That ain't nothin' like a damn persimmon. It tastes like *earwax*, if you ask me," Remington added, taking apparent pride in his discriminating palate.

"Will you two quit yer bellyachin'?" Lou said. She inclined her head and put her hands on her hips. "I'm commencin' to git a tad antsy waitin' to see what you two boys are made of."

Both men drained their cups at a gulp.

"Now ain't that better?" she said languorously, running her hands over herself.

Proctor looked at his mug and smacked his lips. "It may taste like hell, but it sure does pack a wallop."

"Don't I know it," Lou replied. "Now how about we finish you two off?"

Remington stood, but to his surprise had to steady himself on the bedpost. He fumbled with his fly buttons for a long minute, but his fingers refused to respond. He glared at Lou, his eyes cold and narrow. "You slipped us somethin', ditn' you, you little bitch?" he slurred.

"Did I?" she said.

"She put somethin' in the damn whiskey," Proctor said, drooling copiously into his beard. "Puke it up, Jack. Quick."

As the disoriented men each rammed a forefinger deep into his throat, Lou scampered by them. She tore aside the Oriental carpet, turned the iron latch-ring, and heaved open the trapdoor.

Proctor and Remington abruptly stopped retching and had groggily half turned when out of the opening in the floor came flying—as though shot from a catapult—the very large and very angry Mutt, teeth bared and ears flattened tight against his head.

"What in the devil—" Proctor croaked, bewildered, before his words were strangled as Mutt's powerful jaws closed with a gristly crunch on his throat.

In the next heartbeat, from the opening emerged Bandit, holding his rifle. Remington cocked and leveled his six-shooter as best he could, but in his haste and confusion fired wildly, sending his bullet into the ceiling of the cabin. Bandit stood calmly on the ladder, thighs braced against the opening, and leveled the gun. Taking aim as deliberately as if shooting game for their supper, he pulled the trigger. The rifle went off with a tremendous roar, and the blast sent Remington reeling backward against the red-hot iron stove. He slumped down in front of it as Mutt began to amuse himself by shaking the already-dead Proctor like a rag doll.

Bandit climbed out of the floor and looked for Lou, who had taken cover behind the washtub. He picked her up in his arms and held her to him.

"Are you hurt?" he said.

"No, I'm fine. Are you? You feel so terribly cold!"

"Never been better," he said. "Can't say as much for our guests, though. How did you know I'd be in the tunnel?"

"When you stopped pounding on the door, I knew you and Mutt must be taking the other way in. But then I remembered that the trapdoor latches shut when it closes, so I had to figure out how to distract them long enough to let you in."

"And how did you manage that?"

Her eyes sparkled at him in the candlelight. "Let's just say that these two didn't have the tolerance for laudanum that I once had."

"Well done, Lou! I'm so sorry that I doubted you. You were right about these two from the start. You really are a marvel!"

"We're a marvelous *team*," she said. "Divide and conquer."

He laughed. "Have you been reading my *Gallic Wars* again?"

Bandit helped Lou to sit down on the bed. He dragged the men's bodies over to the hole, rolled them in, and listened as each hit the tunnel floor below with a sticky smack.

"Good riddance," he said, looking down. He kicked the men's belongings after them, secured the hatch, and again neatly covered it with the Oriental rug. He gave Mutt a big hunk of deer meat and sat down on the bed next to Lou, who now seemed to have lapsed into a kind of shock.

"Lou?"

"I'll be fine in a minute."

He put his arm around her. "You're trembling, dear," he said, pulling her toward him.

"I . . . I almost lost you."

"I'm still here, Lou. Everything's going to be all right again."

Lou began to weep softly.

He kissed the top of her head. "I understand," he said. "It's all over now."

"I know, but . . ."

He kissed her head again. "Why don't we get back into bed now, and start putting this horrible night behind us?"

She nodded. "I'd like that. Will you keep holding me?"

"Of course I will, dear."

She gave him a weak smile, took off her mountain clothes, and slipped naked under the sheets.

He stripped and joined her, and she pressed herself hard against him, facing him unabashedly in her need to know that he was real and alive and with her still. He put his arms around her.

"Bandit, promise me you'll never leave," she whispered.

"We're a team," he said. He kissed her forehead again and again, until she was fast asleep.

THE NEXT MORNING, BANDIT put the two intruders' belongings into a pile outside and burned them, except for Remington's six-shooter and gun belt, which he kept. Then he fashioned a travois, and he and Mutt dragged the dead men's bodies, one by one, down the tunnel and a few hundred yards beyond the cave entrance. There he rolled them down a sharp slope as a gift to the wolves.

When all this unpleasantness was complete, Bandit returned to the cabin to find the stove roaring and Lou pacing the floor wearing only her moccasins. He popped up out of the opening and gave her a baffled look.

"Not that you don't look fetching," he said, "but why the naked pacing?"

She stopped and turned toward him, and he could see that she had been crying.

"What's wrong, Lou?"

"Those men put a bad scare in me. I'm having a hard time shaking it."

"Naturally. They scared me, too."

"They did not," she said, still pacing. "Nothing scares you. You're the very definition of courageous."

"Courage isn't a matter of not being afraid," Bandit said, stopping her mid-stride. "Courage is being afraid and still doing what you must. And that's what you did last night."

She wiped her reddened eyes. "But why do I keep thinking of what *might* have happened?"

"Because it *might* have ended badly. Just as being left behind by your train might have. But in both cases we survived, Lou. Together."

She stood back and held her arms out at her side.

"Look at me, Bandit."

"I *am* looking at you."

"No, I mean really *look* at me. What do you see?"

"I see a very lovely young lady interrogating me in the nude."

"I mean *inside*," Lou said. "I'm confused. Sometimes I don't know who I am anymore."

"What do you mean?"

"I'm *Lou* now—but when the first train comes, do I go right back to being *Louisa*? Or is she gone forever? And can whoever-it-is ever live in New York again, without thinking every second about"—she wanted to say *you*—"this *place*?" She squeezed her head between her palms. "Do you think I might be losing my mind?"

He peeled her hands away from the sides of her head and held them gently in his. "No, Lou, I don't think you're *losing* anything, and especially not your mind. If anything, you're *finding* something—who you truly are. The person you were always meant to become."

She looked at him in desperation. "But who or what will that be?"

"I can't answer that question—not specifically anyway. But I *do* know for certain that she will be even more lovely than she is right now."

She gave him a skeptical sniff, for a moment sounding again like the old Louisa MacGregor. "How could you possibly *know* that?"

He smiled softly at her. "Consider this," he said. "In fall, caterpillars go to sleep in their cozy little cocoons, probably dreaming all winter about the new spring leaves they'll munch on when they wake up. But when they do wake up, they find—to their surprise—that they've *changed*, and the cocoon that was once so cozy is now terribly confining. It can be a hard struggle for them to wriggle free of it, but they do. And what emerges is a creature more beautiful than any spring flower. That's exactly how I see you. A caterpillar named Louisa MacGregor fell asleep in her palace car, never imagining—when she woke up again—that she would have become a butterfly named Lou."

17

The Senator

Albany, New York

"Chauncey, it's awfully good of you to see me on such short notice," Judge MacGregor said to the senator as he sat down in the great man's paneled office. "Especially considering that you've only so recently taken office, and that you no doubt already have too many things to attend to each day."

"Don't mention it," replied Senator Depew. "It's nothing at all for an old friend and fellow Yale man." He put his cigar—the tenth of his day already—down in a huge crystal ashtray on his desk. "Believe me, Washington isn't anything like Manhattan, which is busy and bustling day and night. Here, it's long periods of boredom punctuated by short bursts of sheer insanity."

"I can only imagine," the judge said. "But if any man can champion the cause of our state, it is you."

Depew nodded gratefully, picked up his box of cigars, and offered it over the desk. The judge looked tempted, but then declined.

"I'd love to join you, but my doctor has advised me to stop

smoking. Though I told him in no uncertain terms that I refuse to become a vegetarian, as he also recommends."

The senator rolled his eyes. "I've been getting the same terrible advice from my physician. Too many cigars. Too much brandy. It's so tedious! A man's got to be allowed a few harmless vices."

"Well said, Chauncey."

"Now, Jim, tell me more about this terrible situation . . . about your Louisa's predicament."

"There's been no progress at all since you and I saw each other at Christmastime," MacGregor said. "I can't blame Bartholomew, really—"

"Believe me, I know how railroad men think," Depew said, puffing on his stogie. "Protect the line at any cost."

"And in this case, the cost was my daughter," the judge said.

Depew nodded gravely.

"Bartholomew *has* promised to send a crew as soon as the season will allow, but it's the not knowing that's the hardest thing. If Louisa is . . . if the worst has happened, we'd at least like to bring her home and lay her to rest with some dignity. It's horrendous to imagine her as . . . well, the wild animals and all that. That's why I asked if Governor Roosevelt might have some idea of what to do, since he knows that country so well."

"I asked him about it yesterday," Depew said, setting his cigar down in the ashtray. "He said, and I quote, that he'd like to strap on a pair of snowshoes and see about it himself. He said that escaping Albany would be the hardest part of the whole journey."

"That sounds like Teddy," MacGregor said.

"The man is fearless. But his own daring aside, he told me in no uncertain terms that Bartholomew is right, and that for all practical purposes, there's no way a search party can reach your daughter's train until spring."

"That comes as no surprise, unfortunately," the judge said with a sigh. "Does he think that the situation is survivable?"

Depew gazed down his cigar, then looked up again. "While it's certainly not impossible, Jim, I think it might be well to prepare yourself and Julia for the worst."

"Yes," the judge said, disheartened. "You're probably right. I do thank you sincerely for looking into the matter. It's a kindness I won't forget, and I trust you will also convey my deep appreciation to TR."

"Our hearts are breaking about the whole thing," Depew said. "And while I recognize that this may not come in time to help with your daughter's situation, Roosevelt and I have rammed through an approval for the Sierra Pacific's request for a giant rotary snowplow locomotive. There's been intense competition among the roads for this new machine, but we steered it toward the SP. And we made sure that Bartholomew understood that its first mission will be to clear the Donner Pass."

"And do you know when that may be?"

"Fingers crossed, they are hoping for March."

"Then that's how it must be," the judge said, standing. "Chauncey, I am sincerely grateful to both of you."

Senator Depew stood and extended his hand. "I know it will be difficult, but I know you well, Jim. You can manage it. And please give Julia my best. You'll both be in my prayers."

"I can't thank you enough," he said, shaking the senator's hand.

"Good luck, my friend. Please do keep me informed."

18

Whiteout

*L*ou was hoping for calmer days ahead, and for a while her wish was granted. Until, that is, one morning when Bandit said, as usual, that he was going out to see if he could hunt up something for supper. They were both getting sick and tired of ham and beans, and a little venison, squirrel, or hare would offer a nice change of pace.

"May I come with you this time?" Lou asked.

"I thought you didn't like hunting?"

"I don't . . . but on the other hand I don't really *know* anything about it. I can't even picture in my mind what it is you *do* when you are gone for hours on end."

"Then you may be my guest. Do you think you can snowshoe well enough?"

"If I get tired, I can always turn back."

"That's the spirit!"

He collected his hunting gear and draped a supple fur cape over her shoulders.

"Where did this come from?" she asked, feeling its wondrous softness.

"From the trapline. It's marten. I wanted to make something warm and light for you. You were ready to collapse under the weight of my buffalo robe."

"It's the most beautiful thing I've ever seen," Lou said. "But I hope at least we'll eat the martens."

"*Well . . .*" he said, "you *can* eat marten, and I tried it once. And that once was enough. They stink to high heaven, and taste even worse. But don't worry—they won't go to waste. I set the carcasses aside for the wolves."

They were about to leave when he went back to their bed and reached under the ticking. He came back with Remington's Colt six-shooter and held it out to her.

"You'd better have this along, just in case."

She took the revolver from him and hefted it. "But this is so *heavy*! Maybe I could take my derringer instead?"

"That's a city gun," he replied. "*This* is what you need out here. But remember, you have to pull back the hammer first to make it go *bang*."

"Very funny."

"I thought so."

They walked out into the cold, where it was still early enough that there was no need for smoked spectacles.

"The sky doesn't look too bad," he said, looking up. He nodded down the valley toward a fold in the landscape. "Let's try over that way. I saw some deer tracks there yesterday."

They shuffled along in their snowshoes for a good half mile. It was exhausting, but Lou refused to make the slightest peep of complaint. *Pretend you're a butterfly, Lou.*

They picked up fresh deer sign at the base of the first long ridge that overlooked their valley. Hiking uphill, they passed through a thick patch of forest and, at the ridgeline, they stopped to take in the view of the encircling ramparts of the mighty Sierras. In the far distance lay another, much wider valley, a long oval of white set with a turquoise-blue lake.

"That lake looks like your eyes," Lou said without thinking.

"Like my eyes?"

"Yes, that bright blue lake with the white around it."

He looked over at her. "You could be a poet, if you wanted to."

All I'd write about is you, she thought. "Well, who knows what the future will bring," she said instead, looking away.

The stiff wind across the crest line had honed the crust of snow into a long row of sharp and brittle teeth.

"Lou! Watch your step!" Bandit said abruptly, putting a hand on her shoulder. "If you get any nearer the edge, I'll have a very long hike to retrieve what's left of you."

"You are so very droll," she said dryly. "I wouldn't want to put you to any trouble."

He laughed. "No *more* trouble, you mean?"

"Laugh all you like, mountain man. But just remember, old Lou could have decided to spend the winter with those two prospectors, and leave you down in the tunnel until spring."

"Point taken," he said.

They stood and gazed out over the massive range, listening to the sigh of the wind rising up from far below.

"It's just so beautiful here," Lou said. "To think that once I thought Central Park was pretty."

"Central Park *is* pretty," Bandit said. "But this . . . is *sublime*. No human hand could design something like this. Only the hand of God."

She pulled her fur cape close around her shoulders. "*God*," she said. "Bandit, do you think there really is a God? I mean, really and truly. Not just Sunday school stories."

"You felt his presence yourself, Lou," he replied. "And I have, too. So yes, most definitely I believe there's a God."

"Mightn't nature itself be God?"

"That's a very interesting question," he said. "One I've thought about quite a bit out here. This place is so powerful that it's easy to think of it as God. But no, I don't think it is."

"Will you tell me why not?"

"Of course! The way I see it—nature is powerful, but it's indifferent. And it can be terribly cruel. And while God is even more powerful than nature, he is neither cruel nor indifferent. He is *loving*."

Lou considered this for a moment. "I've heard that very thing *so* many times, Bandit. But if God is loving . . . then why do such horrible things happen to people? If God loves us, and he's all-powerful, why doesn't he stop them from happening?"

"Well, I certainly can't speak for God," Bandit said, "but I tend to think he loves and respects us enough to allow us to be *free*. How could we be free if he were forever intervening in everything that happens to us? Wouldn't we be only so many puppets? I don't think God wants puppets, Lou. I think instead he wants us to experience what it is to be fully human. And unfortunately sometimes that means feeling very, very bad when bad things happen."

"Like those two awful prospectors."

He nodded, looking at the distant lake. "That's it exactly. The God who created all *this*"—he swept his arm across the span of the Sierras— "surely had the power to strike those two down with the flick of his little finger. And, at the moment, we might have been grateful if he had. But don't we both feel even more wonderful for having survived that ordeal on our own? True, we had to look death in the face, but in doing so we gained a deeper sense of how sweet *life* is. That is both the price and the reward of freedom."

She looked up at him with full eyes and a sudden desire to kiss him. "Bandit, you truly are a beautiful man."

He raised an eyebrow. "And *this* from the same lady who not so long ago said I was ugly."

"I meant beautiful *inside*," she said. "Not that you're too bad on the outside, either."

"For a mountain man."

"For *any* man. Trust me, with your looks . . . if you only had money, you'd turn the head of every young lady in New York."

"Hmm. I wonder . . . how much money would I need? To turn heads, that is."

She thought for a moment. "Oh, I'd say a million dollars would do it."

"That's an awful lot of money," Bandit said, seeming downcast.

"Oh, lots of women's heads would *still* turn if you hadn't a red cent, but if you had a *million*? Believe me—ladies would start following you down the sidewalk."

He laughed. "And *there*, in a nutshell, is the problem with money. It becomes the only thing people can see about a fellow."

"I suppose," Lou said. "Fortunately, you don't have that problem. So I can see you for who you are."

"That is exactly what I hope, Lou."

They stood in silence for another minute. Bandit again glanced up at the sky.

"You know, Lou, I don't like the way the wind is picking up," he said. "It smells like snow is on the way. With any luck, it might turn out to be nothing, but if not . . . I don't want you to be caught out in a blizzard. I'm thinking it might be for the best if you went back to our cabin."

Our cabin, she thought with a start. "Don't you worry about me, big man," she said, making a bicep. "I can handle a little snow."

He shook his head. "A blizzard here isn't 'a little snow.' You're not strong enough on snowshoes yet to handle one. While you're doing very well, we have still to build up those little legs of yours."

"My *little legs*? I'll have you know that I've been told I have especially fine legs."

"They *are* shapely. But not strong enough—not yet. That will come in time."

She stuck out her bottom lip. "So long as I don't get big muscly legs like you have."

"Say, how about we argue about your legs later? Those clouds are getting darker by the second. I think you'd better get a move on."

"What about you? If snow is coming, shouldn't we both go back home?"

"This deer track is so fresh that I want to follow it just a bit longer. But if I don't get a shot within a half hour, I'll come right back."

"Then I will go, but under protest," she said, putting her hands on her hips.

"Your objection is noted. Just follow our tracks back to the cabin, and don't wander off of them, or you'll get lost. Until you know them well, these woods look the same no matter which way you go. And keep that six-gun handy."

"I thought the bears were still asleep?"

"They are, but as you know there are plenty of wolves. I doubt they'll bother you, but better safe than sorry."

"All right." She waved a mitten at him. "Half an hour, now, and no more. Promise me."

"I promise. Now scat!"

He turned and hiked over the ridge and was gone from sight before she'd even started back through the woods to the cabin. *Our* cabin, she thought again, feeling warm despite the cold.

⌘

WHEN BANDIT HAD DISAPPEARED from view, Lou faithfully retraced their snowshoe tracks through the deep and silent forest. With each step, though, the wind picked up. Soon its soft whistle deepened into a moan, then a howl, and then rose again into a weird, keening shriek. The frozen crust atop the snow began to shatter, pelting Lou with sharp chunks. She pulled her scarf up so that only her eyes peeked out under the pert fur cap Bandit had made for her.

At such an altitude, Lou had to stop every ten steps or so and pant for breath. Now the wind, wailing like a banshee, began to jar loose man-sized chunks of snow held aloft by the strong arms of the pines. There was no way to dodge them all, and Lou had the wind knocked out of her by a big one that caught her square on her back. She went down face-first into the snow, and came up wheezing.

In its fury, the uncaged wind began to roar, vengeful and full of malice, making the towering, ancient lodgepoles shudder and quiver like reeds. Just as Lou thought things could get no worse, a vortex of snow—a tornado of white—spun her off her feet entirely. Gasping and squinting, she knew she could go no farther. Earth and sky had become as one, and to wander in such a trackless world was to die. Lou crawled on all fours over to the nearest lodgepole, and curled up against its huge, scaly trunk.

She couldn't be too far from the cave, but with their snowshoe tracks now completely scoured away, it wouldn't be wise to guess its direction. A wrong choice—even only a few degrees off of the right one—could well end in a two-thousand-foot fall.

At first she couldn't conceive of what, if anything, to do next. Her thoughts were as confused as the snowstorm attacking her from every direction at once. Then she remembered something else Bandit had told her: *In the High Sierra, if you don't know where you are going, the best thing to do is to go nowhere.* She pulled herself up into a sitting position next to the big lodgepole, which for a century had withstood the fury of so many of these storms.

Yet despite her layers of fur and leather, Lou was growing desperately cold, and her feet had gone numb and dead. She began to despair that she had come so very far, only to be smothered by snow, frozen to death, and feasted upon by wolves. She tried to summon the will to stay above the rising tide of dread which threatened to drown her in its cold depths, but her spirit and her strength were fast ebbing away.

She sagged weakly against her tree that, she thought wryly, would soon become her grave marker. Clasping her mittens together in prayer, she began to whisper: *Into thy hands I commend . . .*

But then—to her utter astonishment, something inside her flared up—and in an instant burned away every trace of her fear like a firestorm. She began to howl defiance back at the wind, and with all of its own fierce intensity. "You will not defeat me!" she screamed wildly into the storm. "I will live! I *will* see him again!"

Him. Him. *Him.* That little heartbeat of a word soon gave way to another one, equally small and yet at the same time impossibly large. At long last, Lou understood what had been growing quietly inside her, a little bit each day, since she had come to this place. And now, this once-tiny thing had become so enormous that it had taken her over completely, and had replaced the old Louisa with an entirely new creature.

That thing was *love*.

'God is not indifferent—he is *loving*,' Bandit had said only minutes before—and while Lou had had her doubts, even then, now with each choking breath she was filled with all the power and force contained in those simple words. And with this flash of understanding came to her a resolve as unshakeable as the Sierras themselves: that if she must die, she would die *only at his side*. Then, and only then, would she relinquish—gratefully—the life that she had come to love. She had made her choice at last: for life, for love, and for the freedom to feel it all.

She cried out for Bandit. But the howling wind mocked her, and an ocean of snow absorbed her voice as completely as it had obscured earth and sky.

Then she remembered: *the six-gun*! Surely the report of the big revolver would be loud enough to be heard over whatever distance separated them. At his stalking pace, Bandit couldn't have gone far from the ridge where they had only so recently stood and talked of the works of man, of the power of nature, and of the one thing far, far greater than both.

Calm now, Lou shook off her layer of snow and carefully unslung her pack. She pulled off a mitten—in seconds her exposed skin felt as though it was on fire—and reached into the depths of the pack. She fished out the revolver, closed the pack up tightly, and again secured it to her back.

Lou curled her frozen index finger around the trigger of the gun—and then remembered that she had to cock the hammer first. She pulled it back against its spring with the heel of her other mitten.

At last it clicked into position and hovered eagerly over the rear of the cylinder.

Pointing the gun over her head, she closed her eyes and pulled resolutely on the trigger. The thing went off with a report so loud it briefly deafened her. But the tremendous roar of the weapon was reassuring, too. Surely Bandit would hear *that* sound and could navigate toward it!

After a minute or two of impatient waiting, though, there was no sign of him. Lou repeated the procedure, firing another blast into the sky. Two shots gone, she thought. It's a six-gun, so I will have four left. She counted to a hundred and again let fly.

Yet after another hundred count, there was still no Bandit. She fired off another shot. *Come on, Bandit. Come back to me.*

Four shots were gone, and she didn't wait long before letting go with a fifth. And with the blast, the wind seemed to abate, if only slightly. Lou was cheered by the thought that the squall might go as suddenly as it had come—as Bandit had so often told her. Now she could see a little distance through the trunks again; earth and sky were retaking their rightful places. Only one more left, she thought, cocking the hammer. *My last one, Bandit. Come back to me, my—*

Click.

There was no report, only the dull metallic sound of the hammer falling. She pulled it back and squeezed the trigger again—another click. Lou knew it was futile, but she tried again, and again, until the cylinder had rotated all the way around its axis. Then she recalled Jack Remington's wild shot into their ceiling, and could no longer deny that she was out of ammunition. She clutched the dead revolver and told herself that if Bandit hadn't heard five of the big gun's calls, a sixth would do no good anyway.

I'll count to five hundred, she thought. If the wind has calmed by then, and I have some visibility, I'll go looking for him. But then again, no—Bandit wouldn't want that; without a common destination, we might *both* become lost. He would tell me to meet him at the cave, that he could find his way back home. That's where I'll go.

But before she'd reached the halfway point of her count, the grim woods began to brighten. Snow was still blowing sideways, but Lou could now see a good twenty yards. She had reached four hundred when she saw a large, dark shape emerge from the whiteness. At first she thought it must be a bear, awakened by all of her shooting, and she wished that she had at least one more shot in the six-gun. But it occurred to her that no sane bear, even the hungriest of all, would investigate a series of gunshots, and so the shape must be . . .

"Bandit!" she yelled at the very top of her spent lungs. "*Bandit*! Over here!"

"Lou?" came a familiar voice from the lumbering shape. "Call again!"

"Here! Bandit! Here! *HERE*!" she screamed, over and over, until her voice failed her entirely.

"I'm on my way!" he yelled back, and in a minute he shuffled up to her lodgepole pine on his snowshoes, looking nothing at all like a man who'd only recently been lost in a deadly blizzard.

"Good girl!" he said.

She looked up at him, exhausted, bedraggled, and with ears ringing like cathedral bells.

"Good *girl*?"

"*Lady*, I mean to say. You did *exactly* what you should have done. When that squall came on, you stopped. You waited. You were *patient*."

"I *do* listen to you sometimes," she grumbled, though secretly wanting to jump up and smother him with kisses.

He held out a hand and pulled her to her feet. "Using the gun to direct me to you was inspired," he said. "I am so very proud of you. You kept your wits about you."

"I will admit I nearly panicked," she said with a touch of pride. "But I calmed myself down."

"And that's a lesson that only the Sierras can teach you."

She smiled at him, again wanting badly to throw her arms around him as the snow seemed friendly again, falling slowly in great, puffy flakes from somewhere high above. "Not only the Sierras," she said. "You get the credit, too. You're a great teacher."

"Then I am happy. And relieved."

"Were you worried about me?"

"Hmm. At first I was. But then—not really. I was confident that you would do what you needed to."

Lou wished he might have been a *little* more worried, but she reassured herself that his confidence was an even bigger compliment.

"I think we better get on our way before we have another surprise," he said.

"I agree—but in which direction?"

He winked, his eyelashes caked with frozen snow. "Orienting yourself out here will be your next lesson. Soon, you'll know these woods as well as you know the streets of New York."

"But every tree looks exactly the same!"

"As does every Manhattan street—to the newcomer. But soon one realizes they're all quite unique. The same is true about these trees." He looked around for a moment and then pointed. "So, let's see . . . our cave would be . . . *that* way."

They were starting to shuffle off when he stopped her with a big mitten. "Hold on," he said, and began brushing off all the snow that had piled up on her. He reached under her cape and shook out her shirt, loosing a little avalanche.

"What an incorrigible masher you are," she said with mock indignation. "Reaching under a lady's cape without so much as asking permission."

He laughed. "You're not a lady anymore."

"I beg your pardon!"

"I mean . . . you're a *mountain* lady now. And there's no going back from that, I'm afraid."

They trudged off, and after a few yards Bandit threw an arm around Lou's shoulder.

19

Valentine's Day

February 14, 1900

After they had finished their breakfast, Bandit sat down against the bed and began making some repairs to Lou's deerskin trousers, which she had snagged on a tangle of fallen branches during the whiteout.

"You take excellent care of your clothes," he said. "Only a couple small tears. I'm forever fixing mine."

"That's because you're a big ogre, and I'm a lady," she said, extending her bare legs by the stove and turning her body to give him a good look. "Even if I'm now a mountain lady."

"Right on both counts," he said. "By the way, if you don't mind my saying, you look especially pretty this morning."

Mind your saying? Lou thought. Good night. Why would I mind?

"No, I don't mind at all," she said aloud. "I brushed my hair while you were outside splitting wood."

"It suits you very well—over your shoulders like that."

She ran her fingers through her hair, smoothing it so that its tips just brushed along the tops of her breasts. "Would you like me to arrange it like this?"

"Whatever you like is fine by me."

Naturally, she thought.

After a while, he stood up, stretched, and handed her the trousers. "You don't have to put these on, of course," he said with a grin. "But they're good as new."

"I'm fortunate to have an expert tailor on call."

He chuckled and took a look at the calendar tacked up to the wall.

"Say, Lou . . . you'll never guess what today is!"

She walked over and stood next to him, looking at the calendar. "What?" she asked.

He stabbed a date with his fingertip.

"February 14th," Lou murmured. "*Valentine's Day*. Now that *is* special."

She tried to dismiss from her mind the sudden image of a slow, candlelit supper with Bandit, with the wind screeching outside . . . then a kiss, then he would sweep her off her feet and carry her to their bed, right over there, and *then* . . .

"That's not what makes it special, silly," he said cheerfully, bursting her bubble.

Of course not, she thought. "Then do enlighten me—what makes today special?"

He tapped on the calendar page again. "Tonight's the full moon!"

She looked at him with lidded eyes. "Well now, isn't *that* romantic?" she said, trying on a husky, come-hither voice she had been practicing while he was out hunting.

"You sound funny," Bandit replied. "What kind of accent is that?"

She sighed. "I must have had a frog in my throat."

"I have some slippery elm bark for that, if you want some."

"Don't worry—it's gone now," she said, clearing her throat. "Completely."

"Yes, that's better. Anyhow, I've been thinking—you know what we ought to do tonight?"

You better believe I do, mister, she thought.

"I can't begin to imagine. What might you have in mind?" she asked, making doe eyes at him.

"Tonight we should hike over to the top of the ridge and see the mountains by moonlight. It's the most wondrous sight you can imagine."

"But you've said a hundred times we shouldn't go out at night! Maybe instead we could just stay in and . . . *be together*?"

He looked bemused. "We'll be together on our hike."

"That's true, I suppose," she said, quickly cooking up a fallback plan. "Then perhaps I could at least make us a nice supper?"

"Perfect!" he said.

"If only we had some champagne," Lou said. "Valentine's Day isn't really Valentine's Day without a toast."

He looked crestfallen for a moment, but then perked back up again. "While I can't offer you champagne," he said, "I *do* have a bottle of whiskey tucked away in the tunnel. So tonight we will still be able to say 'bottoms up!'"

Ha! Lou thought. You're darn right we will.

"I'll fetch it now," he said. "Don't go anywhere!"

Where does he think I am going to go?

Bandit climbed down into the tunnel. She heard him rummaging around for a minute or two, and then he reemerged, holding aloft a very dusty bottle of whiskey. "Right where I left it!" he said.

Lou padded over to him in her moccasins. "Old Overholt," she said, reading the label. "My father likes that. I'd say that's pretty darn good whiskey for a mountain man!"

"Some mountain men *do* like good whiskey," Bandit said. "In any case, we're all set. We'll have our moonlight hike, some supper, and—for the grand finale—a toast to Saint Valentine."

The grand finale! Lou thought gleefully. Tonight's the night! No man, not even this big lunkhead, can resist moonlight, a home-cooked meal, whiskey—and *a naked woman*. She chuckled to herself, wondering how in the world prim Louisa MacGregor could have changed to such a degree that it was she who had become an eager ravisher of mountain men. What a wonderful thing life is, she thought archly.

Tomorrow morning there will be one less virgin in these mountains!

WHEN AT LONG LAST night did spread itself over the High Sierra, Bandit seemed as excited as Lou was. At around seven o'clock, he darted outside, still naked save for his boots. He returned a few seconds later wearing a broad smile.

"It's already *huge*!" he blurted.

"Huh?" Lou said, looking down. "It looks the same to me. If anything, a little smaller. But I'm sure that's just the cold."

"Not *that*, silly. The *moon*!"

Lou exhaled. "Oh. Yes, of course. The moon."

"Get your clothes on and let's go," he said. "There isn't a cloud in the sky just now, so there's not a moment to waste. We'll be good and hungry when we get back from our hike."

"Wouldn't you rather have a little whiskey before we *put any clothes on*?" she said, attempting a smoky stare.

"I don't think that's such a good idea," Bandit said. "I'd be afraid you might miss your footing if you got a little tipsy."

"On snowshoes?"

"Yes, even on snowshoes. Now get dressed, will you? If we go now, we'll still have all night to frolic when we get back."

All night? she thought, astonished. Maybe after three hundred times, an 'all-night frolic' is a walk in the park. Well, I'll just have to do my best to keep up!

They pulled their clothes on and climbed down into the tunnel.

At the bottom, he took her gently by the shoulders and looked deeply into her eyes. "I predict you'll never forget this night, Lou," he said. "Are you ready?"

"Oh, Bandit," she said, looking steadily back, "I've never been more ready in my life."

Bandit lit the railroad lantern while Lou threw the fur cape over her shoulders, put on her big mittens, and popped her fur cap over her hair, which she had brushed a second time, just for good measure.

Outside, they lashed on their snowshoes and set off toward the ridge overlooking the distant lake, which lay far below their high valley.

The moon was indeed huge. It seemed to Lou much bigger here than it ever had in New York—many times larger—though she couldn't fathom why that would be. And in the clear and cloudless sky, the brilliant orb threw off an astonishing amount of light, so much of it that the railroad lantern was mainly superfluous, except when they had to thread their way through a particularly dense stand of trees.

"Will you just look at that moon—and those stars!" Bandit exulted. "Isn't it *glorious*, Lou? Can you imagine anything more intoxicating?"

Wait until I pour that whiskey down your throat, she thought, and immediately fell into an intoxicating fantasy of her own, in which she and Bandit were engaging in some truly *glorious*—

"Lou? What do you think?"

"I'm not thinking anything!" she blurted. *God, how stupid*, she thought as soon as the words were out of her mouth.

She recovered quickly. "And I was *not* thinking anything precisely because it *is* so intoxicating . . . that it was simply not possible to think. Anything. Er, it's certainly worlds apart from New York."

"Um, now that would be hard to disagree with," Bandit said. "I'll bet you never saw a moon in Manhattan to match this one."

"Now isn't *that* interesting," she said in her huskiest voice. "I was just now thinking the *very same* thing. There must be a *reason* we're thinking alike tonight, wouldn't you say?"

"Coincidence, most likely," he said, and shuffled off again.

They hiked for the better part of a half hour and came to the crest of the ridge. From this vantage point, the teeth of the High Sierra glittered coldly, a phalanx of silver spears arrayed against the starry sky. In the oval valley far below them, by some alchemy the tiny turquoise lake had turned to quicksilver, reflecting the moonlight like a mirror set in an inky black frame.

"Isn't it breathtaking?" Bandit said, awestruck.

"It's even more than that," Lou said, finding her own breathing getting more than a little ragged. "Though if there's a word for it, I don't know what it is. But it makes tonight all the more *special*, doesn't it?" She slipped her arm under his big buffalo robe and around his waist. He looped an arm around her shoulder, and they stood close together, hushed and worshipful in this vast mountain cathedral.

Then Bandit suddenly went down on one knee.

LOU'S HEART ALMOST BURST as a single thought blazed like a comet across her mind. *This is it*—and on Valentine's Day, too! *What a story this will make—"and then, right there, before the very altar of God, he . . ."*

Then she realized he was tightening the laces on his snowshoe. When he had finished, he stood up with an air of satisfaction. "Sorry about that," he said, putting his arm around her shoulder again. "I was afraid I might lose that one."

"We can't have *that*," Lou said. She worked up her nerve. "You know—this will sound funny—but for a minute I thought you were going to *ask* me something."

"That's not funny at all," he said, looking at her in amazement. "In fact, it's another coincidence! Because there *is* a very important question I've been meaning to ask you for quite a while."

All hope is not lost!

"Yes, Bandit?" she said tenderly, squeezing his waist more tightly and looking up into his eyes. "I don't mind saying that I've hoped for some time now you might have something important to *ask* me."

"Really?" he said, looking puzzled. "Huh. Well, what I have been wondering is . . . do you think you'd ever come out here again? I mean, when you're back in New York."

I could shove you off this ridge right about now, she thought.

"I haven't thought about it, actually," she said through clenched teeth. "Do you mean just to see the scenery, or to visit you?"

"I guess I'm not sure what I mean. And I can't say if I'll stay here myself too much longer."

"Why not?"

"You'll laugh if I tell you."

"I won't laugh, Bandit. Why not? Why wouldn't you stay?"

"Because you're a part of this place now, Lou. And when you go, I know it won't—can't—be the same. It will still be beautiful, of course. I'll still have *this*. But I don't think it can ever *feel* the same without you in it."

See, he *can* be romantic, she thought. Maybe he's just shy?

"That's really a very sweet thing to say, Bandit. Perhaps one might say that our spirits have become . . . *joined* somehow?"

"I suppose," he said. "But you know . . . while I never thought I'd say this after three years by myself . . ."

"Yes?" Lou said, looking up at Bandit, his chiseled features bathed in silver light. *Those eyes* . . .

"I must admit I've grown accustomed to having another human being around."

"Well, now that's just swell," she said. She took her arm from around his waist. "You know, I think I'd like to head back now."

He looked surprised. "Are you getting cold?"

"Not especially, no," she said. "Maybe a little hungry. I feel empty."

"Fear not," he said. "Once we have that supper of ours, you'll be nice and full."

I'm beginning to have my doubts, she thought.

⸙

"Happy Valentine's Day, Lou!" he said later, holding up his mug of Old Overholt.

"Happy Valentine's Day to you, too, ogre!" She knocked her mug against his, sloshing a bit of the whiskey over the lip. "Whoopsie!" she said, giggling.

"You might want to slow down on that," Bandit said. "That's your second mugful."

"I'll have you know I'm no lightweight, misther!" she said,

beginning to slur her words. "You think only you mountain folk can hold your liquor. Well, think again!" She took another big swig.

"Hasn't this been a perfectly delightful evening? That incredible view, a fine supper—thanks to you—and now a nice, hot stove and some whiskey!"

"Not *perfectly*," she said, "but the night is still young. To quote you—'bottoms up!'" She raised her mug and polished it off in one swallow.

"Say, you're quite a lot of fun when you drink," he said.

"I'm *always* lots of fun. You just don't notice."

"Sure I notice!"

She set her mug down and gave him an exaggerated pout, sticking out her bottom lip. "You do not. To you, I'm just another . . . human being person thing you've gotten used to having around."

"Oh, I see," Bandit said. "*That's* why you were so quiet on our walk back. Lou, you know I didn't mean it that way. You're not just any old human being."

"Too little, too late, clod!" she said. "You can't reel in a fish that you . . . after it's . . . oh, I don't know exactly. But it's too late. Too *little*, too *late*," she finished in a singsong voice.

Bandit sighed. "Maybe we'd better turn in."

"*No!*" She held out her mug. "We haven't had hardly anything to drink." She pounded the table with her fist. "Another round, barkeep! And make it shnappy!"

"Maybe just a little," he said, pouring.

She squinted into the bottom of her mug. "Hey . . . what's the big idea? I can still see the bottom of this crummy old mug."

"Lou, that's plenty. And you know you're not just any other person here. You're very special to me."

She put her head down in her arms. "You're just saying that," she mumbled into the table, "because I'm upsthet. But you can't hide from *me*, because I . . . um, know the *truth*. And you've missed it by a mile."

"Then do tell me," he said to the top of her head, "what am I missing? At the very least, I ought to know what it is, don't you think?"

"You want to know, do you, lump?"

"Yes, I do, Lou. If I have overlooked something, I certainly didn't do so intentionally."

She scraped her chair back from the table and stood, weaving slightly on her feet. In the yellow candlelight her naked skin looked as though her body had been fashioned of gold.

"*This* is what you're missing," she purred, turning this way and that and spearing him with her most seductive look, which she had saved up until now. Lou put her hands on the table and leaned toward him. She closed her eyes and puckered up her lips.

"Come on, big man. You know you want me as much as I do. Um, I mean—"

"Lou," he said, "this is the whiskey talking."

Her eyes snapped open again. "*In vino veritas,*" she said. "You probably don't know, but that's Latin for—"

"I know what it means," he said, standing up. "And in that spirit, I think it's time we went to bed."

"First sthensible thing you've sthaid all evening," she said in a stage whisper. "Let's *do.*"

He gently put his arm around her waist and aimed her toward the bed, but she whirled around and faced him. She put her arms over his shoulders.

"Do you find me repulsthive?"

"*Repulsive*? You're beautiful. I've told you that many times."

"Actions speak louder than words."

"You can't possibly think it would be honorable for a fellow to take advantage of a woman who's had too much to drink, can you?"

She rubbed up against him, tapping his temple with her forefinger. "Let me ponder that. Umm . . . *yes*. Definitely."

"Well, that's fine for you. I don't think it would be, however, and what's more, we'd both likely regret it. I could never look your father in the eye if I'd done such a thing. Now come on," he said, peeling her arms from around his neck. "Off to bed with you."

Sullenly she flopped onto the bed, stretched out full-length on her stomach.

"Don't bother to get up," he said wryly. "I'll blow out the candles."

"I have to use the pot," her muffled voice said into the pillow.

"I'll get it for you." He brought the chamber pot over to the bed.

"A little privacy, if you please," she said, giving him a mule kick.

"I'm moving as fast as I can!"

After she'd relieved herself, Bandit helped her under the covers and tucked her neatly in. She patted the bed next to her. "What'sh taking you so long?"

He laughed and slipped into bed next to her. Lou flipped onto her side and put her head on his shoulder. "Don't think I'm giving up so easily," she said. "I have not yet begun to fight!"

"You're not the giving up type, Lou," Bandit whispered into her hair. "That's one of the things I love about you."

"Talk is cheap, lump," she said.

"Not with me, it isn't. Remember, I didn't talk much at all for nearly three years. Well, except to the dog, but that doesn't really count since he didn't talk back."

"*Woof*," Lou said.

"Good night, dear," he said. "If you should feel sick to your stomach—"

"I can handle my liquor, pal," Lou said, even though the room was spinning like a top.

"Happy Valentine's Day, Lou."

"Best one *ever*," she said in a sarcastic voice. "I wonder where we'll both be *next* Valentine's Day," she added, much more softly.

"Maybe right here," Bandit said.

"Only if the cabin collapses on us."

"That's not very nice."

She didn't reply, and instead began snoring loudly on his shoulder, reeking of Old Overholt.

20

The Diary

"There's so much I want to remember about this place," Lou said to Bandit one afternoon when they were returning from a successful hunt for winter hare. "Yet I fear I'll forget something."

"Have you thought about keeping a diary?" he asked. "I have a blank book or two in the things I brought from the East."

"That might be fun. Do you have pen and ink?"

"I have a pen, but earlier this season, like an idiot, I left my ink sitting out overnight. It froze solid, and the bottle shattered."

"So much for that idea."

"Maybe not. If you'd like, we can make some ink out of pine cones. It'll be fun!"

"You can do that? Make ink out of pine cones?"

"Oh yes. Now mind you, the result isn't quite so good as the commercial stuff, but it works well enough. And years from now, when you read your diary, or your children read it, you will remember making the ink that wrote its words."

"What a wonderful idea," Lou said. "But I don't think that I'll be letting any children read about this chapter in my life. Imagine! 'Trapped in a sweltering cabin, naked, with a mountain man.' No right-minded person would understand."

"I expect that's so," Bandit said. "And they certainly wouldn't believe that the whole thing had been accomplished chastely, and without a single incident of your dreaded ravishment." He laughed, swinging their rabbits by the feet as they shuffled along atop the deep drifts.

Lou wanted to laugh along, but he had pressed hard on a bruise: Bandit's continued, inexplicable lack of interest in her—as a *woman*—had become as nagging, persistent, and thoroughly maddening as a ringing in the ear.

There's either something wrong with me, or with him, she would think. Even after she had shown such calm presence of mind with the prospectors, and again in the whiteout—which surely would impress any man, especially a frontiersman like Bandit—he still didn't seem to have the slightest interest in a physical connection. He was kind, and tender, and when he touched her it was with a deep warmth; of that she had no doubt. But that was where it seemed to stall—even on her carefully planned Valentine's Day.

Lately, at bedtime, she had begun making a point to wriggle close to him, "accidentally" brushing him with something private. But even this elicited nothing more than a good-natured chuckle or a friendly squeeze, which vexed her all the more.

So this is what I'll write in my diary, she thought, with my home-made ink: "Woke up frustrated again this morning. Spent the day buck naked with a virile, strapping mountain man. Had deep, stimulating conversations and experienced genuine kindness. Went to bed frustrated." *Good night, every single day could be the same entry.*

"Lou?" he said, snapping her out of her trance.

"Huh?" she said, trying to calm her breathing.

"Penny for your thoughts."

"Oh, they're not worth nearly so much."

"When we get home, would you like to make up a batch of that pine cone ink?"

Of all the virile, strapping mountain men I could be stranded with, she thought.

❧

WHEN THEY GOT BACK, Bandit first showed Lou how to gut and skin their hare. Mutt was treated to the innards and eagerly snapped them up. The whole thing disgusted Lou a great deal less than it had as recently as November; by now, she was inured to the sight of blood and guts. It was all just part of surviving each day. The world of the High Sierra was unforgiving and binary—kill or be killed, live or die. If you learned how to kill when necessary, and learned how to live, it could be a beautiful and serene place. If you didn't, something else—a bear, the weather, prospectors, or disease—would indifferently finish you off.

When they were done with the hare, Bandit fetched her a basket and told her to fill it with pine cones.

"Look down near the brook," he said, "where there's not a lot of snow. You'll find plenty of them there."

She foraged around for a while, basking in the soothing serenity of the rushing stream, and reported back to Bandit with a full basket of ponderosa cones.

"Those are *excellent* cones," he said, eyeing the basket approvingly. "Now for the next step."

Inside, he put one of their cooking pots onto the stove and added to it several mugfuls of water. Next he took a handful of washing soda, which they used to keep their clothes and bed linens fresh, and dropped it in.

"Now we add the cones," he said, and she dumped them into the water and soda. He stirred the whole mix together and covered the pot. "And wait." From one of the cabin's shelves he took down a small, empty medicine bottle with a cork stopper and set it aside.

They let the mix simmer for a half hour or so, and it filled the little cabin with the peculiar, characteristic fragrance of the ponderosa pine: mingled cedar and butterscotch. When he deemed the brew to be done, he took the pot off the stove and set it outside to cool. After a few minutes, he brought it back in, and with Lou steadying the little bottle, carefully poured into it a dark brown, oily liquid.

"Voilà!" he said. "Your first bottle of Donner Pass pine cone ink!"

"Remarkable! May I use your pen?"

"Right away, *madame*," he said, and fetched her the pen and the remains of a blank book with most of its pages torn out.

"Was this your diary?" she asked.

"It was . . . from the most difficult time in my life—soon after I arrived here. But a year or so ago, I tore out the pages and burned them. I had learned everything they had to teach."

"I can understand that." Lou smoothed down the next page of the blank book with the heel of her hand, dipped the nib into the bottle, and wrote gracefully in a mellow shade of brown:

Ponderosa pine cone ink made by Bandit and Lou in
the winter of 1900, someplace in the High Sierra.

"See? Works pretty well, doesn't it?" he said, hovering over her shoulder. "Now you can keep your diary."

"Why, thank you, Bandit," she said, turning to look at his handsome face and trying *not* to look at the rest of his body, which had begun to preoccupy her in what she was beginning to think must be a slightly unhealthy way. "You're full of good ideas."

"I think it's that you inspire me!"

If only, she thought. If only.

21

A Man of Sorrows

"Lou?" Bandit said as the first rays of dawn stole through the cabin windows. "Are you awake?"

"Huh?"

She had been dozing in a half-dream in which Bandit was slowly running his hand up her legs, kissing her softly the whole time, and then they would become *one* . . .

"I didn't mean to wake you."

"It's all right."

"I thought I might get up and take Mutt out for a little walk," he said.

"Would you like some company?"

"No, thank you," he responded cheerfully.

"Now that's a fine how-do-you-do."

"I don't mean any offense. I'm craving a bit of solitude this morning, that's all."

"Are you tired of me yapping at you all the time?"

"You don't *yap*—well, not most of the time, anyway—and no, I'm not tired of you. In fact, if you want to know, I've grown rather fond of you."

Fond? she almost blurted out. Instead, she searched for a cleverer way to steer him in a better direction. "Maybe you're just fond of my being naked all the time," she said.

Bandit looked over at her. "As lovely as you are, I can't dismiss the possibility entirely."

"I've been a bit worried about my legs," she said, still struggling to escape her erotic quicksand.

"Why? Is something wrong with your legs?"

"I don't think so," she replied. "But I can't be sure."

He sighed. "I'm completely at sea over here, Lou. Would you mind throwing me a rope?"

"I'm afraid they're becoming big tree trunks like yours. My legs, that is."

"Is that all? No need to be concerned. They're not."

"How would you know? You've never felt my legs."

"Why in heaven's name would I want to feel your legs?"

And now we come to the crux of the problem, she thought. "Because you could tell me if they're getting too big."

"This is silly," he said. "Now if you don't mind, I need to take Mutt out."

"Not until you feel my leg."

He reached over and gave her knee a quick squeeze. "There. Satisfied? May I go now?"

"My *knee* is not my leg, you lump. It's my *thighs* I've been worried about."

"If I feel your thigh, will you let me go on my walk?"

"Uh-huh," she said. "But you have to give it a really good test."

He placed his hand lightly on her thigh, but didn't squeeze it at all. Instead, he stroked it, just as she'd been imagining, along the top, then the outside, and then—looking into her eyes—along the inner part, but stopping just before the apex.

"That feels *so* very good," she murmured. "You have a nice touch."

"That's kind of you to say," he said somewhat lamely. "My hands are probably hard from all the chores, though." An odd look crossed his face, and he tried to turn away quickly, though not quickly enough.

"Well, how now, brown cow," she said, her eyes lighting up. "Why, Mr. Bandit! Speaking of *hard*—it seems you were getting a bit more out of my thigh than you let on."

He looked down at his thing and blushed. "Good grief," he stammered. "It has a mind of its own sometimes."

"It's paying me a compliment," she said softly, looking deeply into Bandit's clear blue eyes. "And who doesn't *love* compliments?"

"Thank you for understanding," he said sheepishly. "Now may I get going?"

Go for the kill, Lou, she thought.

"Yes, yes, you can go," she said. "But first, may I tell you something I was hoping I might write in my new diary? About this very morning."

"Oh, you mustn't do that," he said, looking alarmed. "A diary is supposed to be private."

"True . . . but I would like to make an exception in this case." Her heart was pounding out of her chest. "But you have to promise you won't tell anyone else!"

"I would never do such a thing," he said. "*Ever.* What is it you want to write?"

She mustered up every shred of her courage. "I want to write that this morning, while we were lying here together, you took that big, beautiful thing of yours"—she nodded at his penis, which was still quite erect—"and slipped it inside of me."

"*Lou!*"

"What?"

"Have you lost your mind?"

"Oooh, you!" she said, smacking her hands into the mattress. "Lost my *mind*? I can't even lose my *virginity*."

"Lou, I promised I'd never take advantage of you. And a promise is a promise."

"I give up," Lou said to the ceiling. "Really. *I. Give. Up.* Here we are . . . I'm sprawled out naked in bed, you're rubbing my leg like there's no tomorrow, you've got a raging hard-on—"

"*Lou!*"

"Well, what else do you want me to call it? A woodpecker?"

"That's actually rather humorous," he said, chuckling despite himself.

"Ha ha ha. If it is, it's gallows humor. Look, Bandit, here it is, plain as I can make it. Right now, right here, I am offering you a once-in-a-lifetime, no-strings-attached chance to make me Number Three-Oh-One."

"Three-oh-one?"

"Your *three hundred and first* instance of coition!" she shouted, clenching her fists. "What else could that mean? God, will you look what I've been reduced to—a rounding error!"

"Lou, you really do need to calm down," he said, scooting out of bed before she could restrain him further. He threw on his clothes like a fireman responding to an alarm and clucked to Mutt.

"Yeah, yeah," she said. "Go take your dog for a walk. I'm suddenly finding I need some time to myself, too."

"You are? Why is that?"

She sat up in bed and glared at him. "Never you mind."

Bandit took down his rifle. "All right, I'm going. But make sure you lock the door behind me. I don't want any repeat of that little situation we had with those prospectors."

"Ha!" she said. "If some other prospector happens by, I'll lock it *after* I let him in, because he's going to hit the jackpot."

"Very funny."

"I'm not joking, you lunkhead."

He ignored her comment and went out, letting in a gust of frigid air.

❧

SHE GOT OUT OF bed and sat on the chair in front of the stove, looking at her legs. She ran her fingers through the hair at the top, closed her eyes, and began to massage herself. But after only a few seconds, she abruptly stopped. She found she was simply too angry with Bandit even to fantasize about him.

What in the world is *wrong* with that man? she thought. Or me? I never even let my fiancé *touch* me, though he begged to on more occasions than I can recall. But out here in the wilderness, stronger and fitter than I've ever been and, to top it off, naked as a jaybird, I can't even *coax* a man into sin. And not just any man, either!

Bandit was unusual, and she had known that from the start, but *this* unusual? There has to be a reason, she thought. The man's not a monk. He's had *three hundred instances* of sexual relations!

She wracked her brain yet again for everything she had been told about men who hadn't any desire. *Equipment doesn't work*? No, that's not it. A minute ago, the darn thing was as hard as a hatchet handle. *Married*? No longer. *Doesn't like women*? Ugh, now that would be bad, but unlikely. *Doesn't find me attractive*? Not to pat myself too much on the back, but I'm simply not *that* bad.

Lou stood and began pacing back and forth, thinking. On one of her trips across the cabin, she thought about the steamer trunk, sitting untouched at the far end of the room. He *has* been strange about that trunk, she thought. Maybe there's some dark secret inside that would explain everything?

One thing she knew for certain, though—he had told her, and she had promised, never to look in that trunk. It was his private property—no different from letters in the post—and thus ought to be inviolable. But do city rules even *apply* up here? she wondered. I am, after all, alone with this very odd man a million miles and months away from anything like civilization. What if he's a human volcano, primed and ready to erupt? Shouldn't I know everything I can, if only to ensure that I'm not in danger?

Of course I should, she thought, and resolutely padded back to the far end of the cabin. She stood in front of the trunk, her hand on her chin. *I probably shouldn't. Yet if I don't, I'll never know.* And there's only one solution to the mystery, and that is that he's hiding *something*. It may be small, or it may be large. But it's *something*.

She put her hand on the hasp of the trunk and hesitated. He had been consistently good to her, even when she hadn't deserved it, and he had never pressed her for anything. Not information, not to give up her laudanum until she was ready, not even—heaven knows!—for sex. He had given and never taken from her. He has always been as good as his word, she thought, and I ought to be as good as mine. Yet if I've given my word to someone who's not who he claims to be . . . why, I've given my word to an *illusion*.

Taking a deep breath, she gripped the hasp and heaved open the lid. Inside, a layer of tissue paper was neatly laid atop the contents, and she pulled it crinkling to one side.

At first glance, the trunk seemed to contain mostly wardrobe items. On the very top was a men's business suit. Lou felt the material between her fingers—expensive and, to judge from the fine, even needlework, looked to be tailor-made. Under it, tucked along the long edge of the trunk, was a very fine ebony walking stick with an ornate gold and ivory handle. *What in the world?*

She gingerly moved the suit out of the way and found under it another one. This one was all in black: mourning attire—deep mourning, its profound darkness unrelieved by a single stitch or speck of anything but purplish-black. It gave her a chill.

Under the mourning suit she found a small, oblong chest made of what appeared to be rosewood. It had its own little hasp and lock, but the key was in it, and with a soft click opened easily. Inside were an assortment of cuffs and collars, and a set of studs and cuff links made of heavy gold and set with large and exceptional Burmese rubies. She lifted out the little tray they were in, and under that found an envelope, trimmed with a deep black border. *A death announcement.* She set that aside.

Underneath it she found a framed photograph of a very beautiful young lady, perhaps in her mid-twenties and wearing the latest styles of a few years before. She was looking at the camera with a look that any woman would recognize—the look of a woman very much in love.

His wife!

Lou suddenly felt a choking surge of shame and guilt, standing there nakedly peeping at these remains of what must have been Bandit's previous life, and the source of the deep sadness he seemed to carry within him. She had known it to be very wrong, but out of hurt and anger had willingly invaded the only private place he still had, the place where he stored away all his pain.

A man of sorrows, and acquainted with grief, she thought with a pang. *Oh my. Oh no. What have I done?*

Hurriedly she tucked away the photograph, the card, and then put the little tray of ruby jewelry back on top. She closed the lid of the rosewood chest and was about to replace it in the trunk when the cabin door creaked open.

She had forgotten to lock it as instructed. Lou whirled around.

"Oh, mountain lady!" his familiar voice called out merrily. "You forgot to lock the—"

When he stepped into the cabin, he glanced first toward the stove, where he thought she might be sitting. In that brief instant, Lou was consumed by an odd urge to jump into his big trunk and pull the lid shut over her. But even that would have been too late. Bandit turned and saw her standing in front of the open trunk, naked, holding his rosewood box in her hands.

22

❧

Wives and Fiancés

B andit's smile fled, and his cheerful expression drained away like water poured on sand. In a fraction of a second, like the briefest flash of lightning, his eyes opened with surprise, then narrowed with anger, and then—worst of all—softened again into deep, bottomless disappointment.

"I forgot my mittens," he said. "It was colder than I thought, so I figured I'd come back for them."

"Bandit," she said, still holding the rosewood box in front of her, "this is not what you think."

"That's good to hear. I thought for a moment you might be looking through my personal things."

He picked up his big fur mittens from where they sat by the stove, and she could tell that he was trying not to weep. She set the rosewood box down and ran over to him.

"Please, *please* don't hate me," she pleaded. "I'm sorry. From the second I opened it, I knew it was wrong."

"Oh, I could never hate you, Lou," he said sadly, hanging his head. "But I think we both deserve a little better than for you to say you didn't think it was wrong *until* you opened it."

"Yes, you're right, of course. I know—knew—it was wrong. It's that after you left, I began wondering—"

"Then you need wonder no more," he said. "I sincerely hope you found whatever you were looking for. And please, be my guest and finish up your search—I'm going out."

"*Please* don't leave," she said, tugging at his sleeve. "Let me explain. Let me make it up to you."

"I don't need you to *explain*," he said. "Nor really do I want you to make anything up. Now, if you don't mind, I would like to be by myself for a while."

"You'll come back, won't you?"

He gave a little snort of scorn. "What else would I do? I'm not about to wander off and die in the snow because you don't know how to keep your hands to yourself."

He walked out in a gust of wind, and the door banged shut behind him.

Lou ran over to the bed, where he had so recently pledged to protect the most intimate secrets of her diary—only to have his own trust violated in return. She threw herself down on the mattress. On the nightstand, the Bible they sometimes read to each other stared at her accusingly. She thought of Judas, and Saint Peter, and all the other small, selfish people who had betrayed the great and the generous—the very best ones of all—to protect their own interests.

She wept bitterly.

⁓

LOU LAY ON THE bed and cried for quite some time, until her eyes were red and sore and she hadn't anything left in her. Then she dressed; for the first time in a long while, she was ashamed of her nakedness.

She carefully repacked Bandit's steamer trunk, closed the lid quietly, and returned to the woodstove, where she sat, staring into space.

Everything seemed to have been turned upside down. Even the cabin seemed less like a cozy paradise and more like the cold world she had left behind: a place of disappointment, suspicion, and deceit; a place where one's word was one's bond only for so long as it was useful. And it was *she*, and she alone, who had invited these evils into their charmed circle—all because of her inability to be *satisfied*. And with searing clarity she understood that what had made this place an Eden had been from the very beginning the simplest thing of all, and yet also the most fragile—a thing called *trust*.

She sat there for a long, long time. At some point, her thoughts simply fizzled out. There was nothing left to think, and nothing left to look forward to. Even the expectation of his return did not bring with it her usual happy anticipation, for she knew that she had opened a gulf between them.

Things had changed.

———

HE DID AT LAST return, as the shadows were beginning to lengthen. He eased in quietly, bringing with him an equally quiet manner— without any of his usual rousing good cheer, but also without any trace of anger, or coldness, or anything. Just *nothing*, as if the man under the big buffalo robe had vanished.

He took off his boots, hat, mittens, and buffalo robe, and sat down to warm himself in front of the stove. But this time he didn't take off his union suit, as usual; that he left on, and he seemed not to notice that Lou was wearing her deerskin and denim. Or if he did notice, he made no remark.

She looked over at him from the bedside and smiled; he smiled back, again without any apparent animosity—but again without anything else, either.

After ten minutes of silent staring at the flames through the isinglass windows of the woodstove, she decided that if this rupture were to be repaired, there was no time to waste in making amends, and it was on her shoulders alone that the burden rested.

"May we talk about what happened earlier?" she asked into the thick silence.

"We can talk about anything you like."

"I violated your trust," she said. "And I did so in full knowledge that what I was doing was wrong. I wish I could go back in time and do differently. Since I can't, I humbly offer you my sincere apology, and I ask for your forgiveness. Now, I wouldn't blame you a bit if you—"

"Lou," he broke in, holding up a hand, "There's no need. I accept your apology."

She almost jumped into his lap. "Oh, Bandit, you can't imagine how—"

"Now *forgiveness*, on the other hand, is a different thing."

"Please, please don't say it!" she said, clasping her hands and going down on her knees next to him. "I will beg if I must. I'll *grovel*. If you can only find it in your heart to forgive me, everything will be all right again."

"Lou, please," he said, helping her back to her feet. "I don't want you to beg for *anything*, not ever. And certainly not grovel. Believe me, if it were in my power to grant you forgiveness, I would do so gladly. But forgiveness is something that can come only from God—and from inside yourself."

"That can't be! If you would only say that you forgive me—"

He shook his head. "When a person asks another to forgive him, really he's asking an innocent party to shoulder a part of his burden of guilt. That may ease it temporarily, but it never lasts. And it can even lead to a kind of contempt for the innocent person who is only trying to be generous and kind. You know as well as I that when Christ forgave someone, he said not only 'your sins are forgiven' but also 'go and sin no more.' To me, that suggests that *true* forgiveness has two parts . . . accepting the wrong you did—and changing your behavior. And no other person can do *either* of those things for any of us, Lou. Therefore . . . only *you* can forgive yourself."

She looked down at her fur-lined moccasins, which had been for so long a source of such pride. "I don't know if I can *ever* do that," she said quietly.

"Dearest Lou," he said, taking her hands in his, "I know a thing or two about how difficult it can be to forgive oneself, especially when you feel that you've injured someone that you . . . care about. We all have to come to peace with that kind of thing in our own time and on our own terms. But as for you and me . . . we're right as rain. We all make mistakes."

She threw her arms around his neck. He kissed her hair, and she wept softly into his shoulder.

LOU HAD EXPECTED TO have nightmares after that horrible incident with the trunk, but her sleep that night was as deep and blissful as any she could remember, even better than in those early days when the laudanum seemed like magic in a bottle. The next day, they rose with the sun, as usual, had their coffee and breakfast, and to Lou's delight Bandit said that he didn't need to go hunting that day—that there was still plenty of frozen meat in the box in the tunnel.

Instead they sat together in front of the fire, something she had once found so boring but which now seemed like the most exciting thing she could imagine.

"Tell me, Lou," he said with his could-be smile. "What exactly did you hope to find inside my steamer trunk?"

She felt a quiver of fear, thinking he might be angry after all.

He read her mind, and he reached over to put his hand on her arm. "Don't worry—it's water under the bridge. But you said that you had questions about me, and I think it's high time I answered them directly. And I *have* been a little too mysterious about that trunk. Anyone in your shoes—er, moccasins—would be curious."

Lou shrugged. "*Curious*? Yes, of course. But I was mostly *angry*—with you and with myself. I simply couldn't fathom why you wouldn't make love to me, even when I was throwing myself at you. I felt completely ridiculous. The more I thought about it, the more I thought that there must be some secret you were concealing. And I had to find it out for myself."

He watched the flames for a moment. "Honestly, I can't blame you for any of that," he said. "I'll be the first to admit that my views about the subject of sexual relations are a little . . . out of the ordinary, compared to many men. Or at least a little out of fashion."

She was tempted to say *I'll say!* but refrained. "Thank you for being kind to me, Bandit," she said instead. "Even though I haven't deserved it."

"You *always* deserve kindness, Lou," he said. "It's your right. Now let's talk about what's in that trunk. I know you found my cuff links and so on."

"I did."

"Those are from my New York days. And you saw the photograph?"

"I did."

"You probably guessed that was my wife. And my mourning suit is in there, and the other clothes are also from my old life. Since I lived and worked in Manhattan, I had to have city attire—not my mountain duds."

She laughed. "No, those might attract some attention in Times Square."

"To say the least. What else?"

"The walking stick threw me. Such a fine item is the hallmark of a wealthy man. And, well . . ."

He coughed into his hand. "I don't seem especially well-to-do."

"Not to put too fine a point on it, no."

"The stick was a gift from my father," he said. "It had been in his family for quite some time. When I left home, he wanted me to have it."

"It's gorgeous. It's the nicest one I think I've ever seen."

"Thank you. I was always proud of it when I would go out walking. I guess I am still proud of it—because I do love my family, and it reminds me of them."

They sat in silence for a little while.

"Would you tell me something about your wife?" Lou said, immediately doubting whether she ought to have asked such a question. But Bandit didn't seem to mind.

"What would you like to know?"

"What was she like? How did you meet?"

Bandit looked at his empty ring finger, smiling almost to himself. "Her name was Emma, and, like you, she was very kind and came from a very good family. She and I met on the carousel in Central Park— well, I should say we were introduced by a mutual friend at the carousel. I think it's fair to say that for both of us it was love at first sight. We were married within a few months of our introduction."

"That's so very romantic," she said, trying to force down an upswell of jealousy.

"You know, it was. Like a lot of young men, I hadn't given much thought to *love*. And so it took me quite by surprise. But when love shows up at your door, however unexpectedly, you have to let it in."

She looked back at him, startled. "It seems you're quite the poet yourself, Mr. Bandit," she said.

He smiled. "You can teach an old dog *some* new tricks, you know."

I'm not so sure about that, she thought. She shook off another emerging fantasy and cleared her throat. "Now then. Do I take it that after your wedding, you and Emma remained in New York?"

"We did. I was working in an office downtown, and Emma was attending nursing school." He looked into the fire, his eyes glistening. "Those were *good* days, Lou."

"To be *newlyweds*," she said, "and in New York. What could be more perfect?"

He blinked. "I thought so. I had an enviable position. Emma was doing very well in school . . . and on the weekends we were entirely carefree."

"It sounds wonderful, Bandit. I'm happy you had that time in your life."

"As am I. But—as these things seem to go—it wasn't meant to last. We'd see happy young couples in the Park with their little ones . . . and naturally we began to think about a family of our own. But there was one little hitch! The nursing school required a student to leave if she became pregnant. Emma would have done so gladly, but I knew how much she'd dreamed of becoming a nurse. And so, one evening over supper, I said that we were still young and had all the time in the world to start a family. I urged her to finish school and do a bit of nursing first."

"That makes sense. And did she?"

"She did, but . . . that's when things went against us. Soon after her graduation, she was assigned to a contagious disease ward, where she contracted scarlet fever."

"Oh no," Lou said.

"I'm afraid so. It ate her up. In two weeks she was gone."

Lou blinked and looked away. "My God, Bandit. I don't know what to say."

He sighed. "There's nothing *to* say. But I will admit that I was completely unprepared for her to die at such a young age, and with so much ahead of her. And us."

"It's a terrible tragedy," Lou said, touching his arm.

"It was, and as you may imagine I blamed—*blame*—myself for encouraging her to keep working—a decision that cost her her life. If I hadn't urged her to stay in school, she might well be alive today. *Probably* would be alive." He wiped his eyes with the back of his hand. "And that's why I know how difficult it can be to forgive oneself. Because after three long years up here, alone with my thoughts, I *still* haven't managed to do it."

Lou moved her hand down his arm and clasped his hand.

"Bandit," she said, "have you ever considered . . . that perhaps you might not *want* to forgive yourself?"

He looked baffled. "Why in the world would I not want to forgive myself?"

"Because now it's you who puts me in mind of that butterfly you compared me to. Being imprisoned—whether in a cocoon of silk, or one made out of guilt—may be terribly *confining*, but it is *comfortable* . . . because it's familiar. To escape means to venture out into the unknown, where every joy is fleeting and where we will probably again be hurt, or again hurt others. The only way to guarantee that we'll never feel any of that is to stay in prison, and refuse to grant ourselves the freedom to be—how did you put it?—fully human."

"Lou," he said, "how is it you are able to apply my own lessons so much more wisely than I can?"

She leaned over and kissed his cheek. "Because we can see things in each other that we can't see in ourselves. That's why we make such a good team."

"That's awfully nice to hear."

"Now if I may, I'll take it a step further," she said. "When I made my little, um, mistake with your trunk, what did you tell me? You said that I always deserved kindness. And so do you. You loved Emma, and she loved you. You both made the best decisions you could—out of love. If I told you that I had urged my husband to keep doing something he loved to do, and it turned out badly, I'm quite sure you would tell me that I had acted only out of love for him and with his happiness in mind. Wouldn't you?"

"Yes, I suppose I would say something like that."

"Then what's sauce for the goose is sauce for the gander, mister."

He smiled at her, his blue eyes full and bright again. "You know something, Lou? You're impossible to argue with."

"I'm not quite sure how to take that," she said with her light laugh. "But I *am* sure that it's time for us both to start living again. Let's both choose to be free together, Bandit."

He reached over and took her hand in his, and they sat by the fire for a long while, lost in thought.

⁓

AT LAST BANDIT HAD to let go of Lou's hand and add some more wood to the fire. When he sat down again, he gave her a little wink.

"Now that you know most everything there is to know about *me* . . . I wonder if you would tell me something more about *you*?"

"You already know everything about me!"

"I do not."

"Well, then, what is it you want to know about Louisa, now Lou, MacGregor, that you don't already?"

"I've told you something about my wife, but I don't know anything about the man who loved you enough to ask you to be his. Your fiancé."

"Where shall I begin?"

He squinted into the fire. "Mostly, I'd like to understand what kind of man could win your hand."

Lou closed her eyes. "I'll do my best," she said. "First of all, his name was Henry. Henry Hannington."

"*Hannington*," Bandit repeated. "Old money."

Lou looked surprised. "Why, yes. Very."

"And what was he like? What did you love about Henry?"

She considered this for a moment. "I loved that he was a gentle soul, very kind, and very misunderstood. As you know, he came from a very great family, but because he was by nature quiet and a bit bookish, he didn't enjoy being in society circles. But his parents weren't having any of *that*, because to be a Hannington is to *be* society."

"Wealth and status can be very confining," Bandit said. "As strange as that may seem."

"I know that now. And I feel free of all that here, especially being with you. A regular fellow, not some society swell."

"Which is all I aspire to be—a regular fellow. Now do tell me, though, what do you think Henry saw in *you* that would inspire him to stand up against his entire social class? That is *not* an easy thing to do in the Four Hundred."

Lou thought about this for a minute. "He thought I was pretty. He used to say that he liked my laugh, and that I was the only person who could make *him* laugh. He often told me that he felt like a completely different person when he was around me."

"Different? In what way?"

"Happier, I suppose. That's what he said, anyway."

"That's high praise," Bandit said.

"And you know, I thought so too—at the time. But now—if I ever do become a wife—I think I'd like my husband to feel like *himself,* whoever that may be. And I've also come to the conclusion that no one can *make* someone else happy—one has to find one's own happiness within, and trust the other to do the same. As with forgiveness, I think happiness is something no one but ourselves can grant."

"That's a very wise statement," Bandit said.

"If it is, it's come at a price," Lou replied.

"How so?"

She took a deep breath. "I told you that my engagement was broken off, which it was. What I haven't told you—because for a very long while I was ashamed to—is that Henry died soon after the engagement was annulled, or whatever the horrible word was. He jumped from the Long Island Ferry. People said it was an accident, but I know better. And I blamed myself for his death."

"Oh Lou," Bandit said, squeezing her hand gently. "I am so very sorry. My deepest condolences."

"Thank you," she said. "I think I might have handled things better if it had been anything but suicide. That left me both terribly sad and very angry. I suppose it still does, although now I don't blame myself for it. I know for certain that his family loved him, notwithstanding their disapproval of his choice of *me* as his fiancée. And I loved him, too. Poor Henry just couldn't love *himself.* And that was an even greater tragedy than his suicide, if such a thing is possible—because I think his soul died long before his body did."

"I can understand that, Lou. Thank you for sharing that with me. It took a great deal of courage."

"Someone I know once told me that courage isn't a matter of not being afraid, but instead a matter of being afraid and still doing what you must."

"Will you stop using my words against me?"

"Take it as a compliment, ogre."

"And so I shall. Yet whatever I may have said, you've been an especially courageous lady this whole time," he said. "Quitting the laudanum, dispatching those prospectors . . . so many things."

"Not too shabby for a rich, persnickety city girl, eh?"

"Not shabby at all."

"You know what I'd like to do now, now that we are both shaking free of the past?" she asked. "I'd like to go outside with you and take in the *present*. Bandit, I want to start noticing all those miracles I've been overlooking. I have a lot of catching up to do."

"Lou, I'd like nothing better. Yet if I may say—I think I have been overlooking one myself."

"Surely not *you*, Mr. Philosophical Mountain Man!"

"I'm afraid so," he said.

"And what is this miracle you've been overlooking?"

He leaned over and brushed his lips against her ear. "*You*," he said softly.

Fever

When February's fury was at last spent, Bandit and Lou's high, secluded valley experienced a surprising warm spell, and they took advantage of the respite to take long walks in the soaring mountains. Generally, they would follow their creek either uphill or down. In the event of another unexpected squall or blizzard, the stream would provide an easy way to navigate back to their cabin.

On a bright morning early in March, the pair first walked downstream and were surprised to find that what had been a small pool in the trickling creek had widened into quite a large pond. Since there was no prospect of going farther in that direction, they trudged back uphill.

"It's most definitely above freezing," Bandit said, wiping his forehead. "I wore too much stuff."

"So did I," Lou agreed, panting with the altitude and exertion. "How about we stop for a little bit and catch our breath?"

"Don't mind if I do."

They sat down on a big rock, which only a few days before had been entirely covered with snow. Today its top was bare and dry.

"Feels good to rest," she said. "Although this view never gets tiring."

"Do you think you'll miss it when you are back in Manhattan?"

"Of course I'll miss it. Although there are things about Manhattan I miss, too."

"Like what?"

She thought for a moment. "Museums. The theatre. Lectures. What I *don't* miss is the endless social things that young ladies have to participate in."

"Maybe you crave solitude more than you imagined."

"That's most definitely another thing this place has taught me," Lou said. "What about you? Do you ever miss Manhattan? It's been a long time since you've been in the city."

"I do miss New York sometimes. Mostly I miss the *ease* of the place. For all its majesty, surviving in these mountains is hard work. In Manhattan, if you have enough money, everything is done for you. Sometimes it would be nice not to have to think about where my food is coming from, or my water, or mending my clothes."

"I honestly don't know how you've managed it all on your own."

He laughed. "Truth is, I don't know, either. One day at a time."

"Have you caught your breath yet?" Lou asked. "I'd like to go a little more uphill before we return home."

"Will you look at you! You're tougher than I am these days. But yes, I've caught my breath—though I'm dry as dust. First let me refill my canteen."

Bandit bent down over the clear, rushing stream and held his canteen under for a bit. He took a deep drink of the icy water.

"Ahh, now that's refreshing," he said, holding out the canteen. "You?"

"No thanks. I'll wait awhile."

"Good training. You know the Indians could go for many miles without any water at all." He took another long drink. Then they hoisted their packs again and set off uphill, laughing and chatting.

The creek came to a rocky outcropping where the implacable boulders had forced the watercourse to turn almost at right angles before continuing to make its way downhill.

"What in the world is *that* thing?" Lou said, pointing to a jumble of branches in the eddying water.

Bandit put his hand above his eyes. "I hope it's not what I think it is," he said quietly.

"It looks like the legs of a department store mannequin," she said.

They ventured a little way into the stream on the rocks protruding above the rushing water. After only about ten feet, there was no mistaking what the object was that was trapped in the tangle.

"My God," Lou said, "it's a *body*. Well, part of one."

There were two human legs, close together, and part of an abdomen, trapped in the snag. Ribbons of entrails were floating out into the current.

"It *would* have to be the *lower* half," Bandit muttered under his breath. He turned to Lou. "That's not just *any* body. It belongs to one of our friendly prospectors."

"How do you know?"

"I tied their feet together before I rolled the bodies down the hillside. And those lashings are still in place."

"Yes, I can see them now," Lou said. "But how in the world did he get *here*?"

"Wolves tore him apart, I expect. They may have dragged this part of him here."

She looked in horror at the decaying remains. "What do we do now?"

Bandit unslung his canteen, unscrewed the cap, and emptied the contents out onto the rocks. "Hope for the best."

"What does that mean?"

"It means that I'm thankful that you weren't as thirsty as I was down below. It's always a risk here, especially in the warmer weather, that somewhere just upstream is the carcass of something. A deer, weasel, could be anything. In this case it's a very bad man, but the end result is the same: a rotting body that can poison a stream for miles. And I just drank at least a pint of it."

"*Bandit*!" Lou said in terror. "Will you get ill?"

He shrugged. "Who can say? Probably."

She stared at the prospector's remains and then looked back at Bandit.

"Try not to worry, dear," he said. "These things happen. They don't always turn out badly."

"I don't want to walk any more," she said, near tears. "I want to go back *home*. Back to our cabin."

"And that's what we'll do, as soon as I drag what's left of *him* out of our stream."

"Don't do that!"

"I have to, Lou, or he'll contaminate the whole creek. There's a ford just ahead where I can wade in and free him from those branches. You wait right here—it won't take me long."

"I'm coming with you."

He shook his head. "You know I always love your company, but in this case it's not a good idea. I've already been exposed to whatever is in that water. If I get sick, that's bad enough. But if we *both* get sick, we are in serious trouble. So you need to stay healthy, just in case."

Lou watched him go—his strong legs propelling him uphill and the sway of his broad shoulders underneath his buffalo robe. Perfectly healthy, she thought—for now. But perhaps inside that perfect body is something unseen and terrible, swarming and multiplying.

BACK AT THE CABIN, Bandit went about his usual chores without any apparent ill effect from the poisoned water. After a while, he sat down and began writing out something with their pine cone ink.

"How are you feeling?" Lou asked, for about the hundredth time.

He put the pen down. "Lou, you've been asking me that every two minutes."

"I'm worried!"

"Worrying won't do any good. We're just going to have to wait and see. Maybe you could write a little in your diary? That's what I'm try-ing to do."

She gave him a pretty little pout. "All I'd be writing is how worried I am about you."

He laughed, and they were quiet for a few minutes.

"Perhaps you'd like to take a nap?" she said.

"I'm not tired."

"May I make you a nice cup of tea?"

"*Please*, Lou."

She got up and paced back and forth along the length of the cabin. With the warmer temperatures and the interior of the cabin blazing hot after their return, she had, as usual, shucked everything except her moccasins.

"You know, if I haven't told you before, your naked pacing is simply adorable," he said.

"Stop that kind of talk, you insensitive lout, until you're ready to put your money where your mouth is!"

"You mean I can't even flirt with you now?"

"That's exactly what I mean. We're *all* business now, pal. You blew your chance."

He laughed so hard that he began to cough, a deep and dry cough.

"Why are you coughing?"

"Because I'm laughing. You're hilarious!"

Midday came and went, and Bandit seemed still to be in good shape, except that he'd had no appetite for their lunch, which was very unusual.

"You have to eat," she had said.

He held his stomach. "I'd like to, but I feel a bit queasy."

The queasiness intensified until—about eight hours after drinking from the stream—Bandit began vomiting. As he had very little in his stomach, after the first time or two only a little bile came up, and then nothing at all but dry heaves.

"I guess we have our answer," he said between bouts of retching. "You still feel all right?"

"Don't you worry about me. I'm fine."

"Thank goodness for that." He gave her a wry smile. "That damn prospector is going to kill me after all. He couldn't manage it the first time around, so now he's having his revenge."

"Don't you say that!" Lou chided him. "We have to think positively."

"It was only a bit of a joke. You're the one who said she likes gallows humor."

"Well, not this time, I don't. So cut it out!"

"Do you know how very pretty you are when you're angry?"

"What did I just say about flirting? Are you telling me that you're ready for the big event?"

"However tempting that may be, I couldn't manage it now even if I tried. I'd throw up on you."

"At my current level of desperation, it would almost be worth it," she said. "Do you have any earthly idea how hard it is to live in a cabin all winter, naked as Adam and Eve, with a man who looks the way you do—and not get any real relief?"

"No, I can't say that I do."

"I didn't mean it literally, you bumpkin."

The diarrhea started a few hours later. Lou had to help Bandit on and off the chamber pot until, in the wee hours of the morning, the cramps eased somewhat. But by that time Bandit was pale and weak, and nothing like his usual robust self.

"You ought to put me out in the snow," he said. "I could make a mess out there at least, and it would be a lot cooler."

"I couldn't even if I wanted to. It's started snowing like mad, and the door's already blocked. I've had to go down into the tunnel to empty the pot."

"So that's why you're wearing your outdoor gear," he said. "Be careful down there, will you?"

"I know every inch of that tunnel now," she said. "Maybe you could get a little sleep? I'm thinking that the worst of it may have passed."

"I certainly hope you're right, but I'm not so sure. Perhaps it *is* a good idea to lie down. Will you stay with me?"

"Of course I'll stay with you."

"Where would you go otherwise, I suppose."

"Even if all of Manhattan were at my feet—or even Truckee—I wouldn't leave you, you . . . lump," she said, choking back tears. "Now shut up and get some rest."

"That's my Lou," he said, and closed his eyes.

She slipped into bed next to him, trying to will him back to health. Lou thought to pray, but the words wouldn't come, so instead she lay there listening nervously to his every breath.

He awoke in the middle of the night and rolled out of bed with a thud. "Whoops," he said.

Lou slid out of bed and helped him onto the chamber pot. After ten full minutes of agonizing cramps, he was at last able to haul himself off of it. When Lou went to empty it, though, she found to her surprise that it was almost full of water and mucus. *Where is all this coming from?* she wondered. The man's had nothing to eat or drink for an entire day!

When she returned with the empty pot, he was slumped forward, with the blanket pulled over his head and was shivering violently. He looked up at her with glassy eyes, his wavy hair falling lank and wet over his forehead.

"You're sweating to beat the band," she said.

"Y-yes," he said, his teeth chattering. "But I f-feel like I'm freezing to death."

She put her wrist against his forehead.

"You're burning up."

"That's comforting."

"What I don't understand," Lou said, "is that the chamber pot was almost full with liquid."

He nodded. "That's because I have dysentery."

"But you haven't eaten a thing!"

"Doesn't matter. That's what dysentery does—it sucks all the moisture out of the body. That's how people die."

She gave him some water, and he managed a few sips. A minute later, though, he vomited even that up again.

Lou filled a bucket with snow and some clean rags and, when the snow had melted a little, laid the cold, wet cloths on Bandit's forehead.

"We've got to cool you down somehow," she said.

Bandit could scarcely stay off the chamber pot now, the cramps filling it again and again with precious body moisture.

"I need a new plan," she muttered to herself after another climb up the ladder.

"Is that you, Louisa?" he said when she popped up through the trapdoor.

Louisa?

On the bed, Bandit now seemed to be slipping in and out of consciousness.

"Louisa," Bandit repeated, clutching her hand with surprising strength.

"Yes, honey? I'm here."

He seemed to collect all his strength. "If I don't make it . . ."

"Stop talking like that," she said, shaking him. "Of course you are going to make it!"

"I hope so. But in case I don't . . . I want you to listen to me very carefully."

"I'm listening."

"I wasn't lying to those men about the valuables. In the tunnel, a little way to the left, behind a big rock, is a Gladstone bag. In it you'll find some money, in case you need it. And there is a document in there that is very, very important. Do *not* lose it!"

"I promise I won't, Bandit," she said. "Don't give it another thought. Now you rest! I'm going to get you some help."

"Don't you *dare* go anywhere," he croaked. "*Donner Party*, remember? This country does not forgive or forget. Just hunker down, like you did in the snowstorm. You've learned how to survive, and the thaw will be here soon. If I don't make it, roll me outside where I won't stink up the place. Like you did with the thunder mug on our first day together."

"Shut up, you," she said. "And besides, you were the one who stunk up the place." She started pacing again, trying to think of what to do next.

"A very good day to you, madam!" he said suddenly, and in a very formal tone.

"Yes, Bandit?" she responded, returning to his side.

"It's delightful to see you again, Mrs. Astor. Have you met my darling Louisa?"

"You're delirious, dear," she said to him. "You're thinking about our first day together, when we talked about Mrs. Astor. And the Four Hundred."

But Bandit had already lapsed into unconsciousness. She studied him for a minute. *Now think, Lou. We have two problems: the diarrhea and this fever. Either one could kill him. Somehow I have to treat them both . . .*

"Medicine," she said aloud, as though he could hear her. "We need to get you some medicine."

Then she remembered that her palace car had been supplied with a full medical kit. When dawn comes, she thought, I'll hike down to the tracks and retrieve the kit. Surely there will be *something* in there for fever and dysentery. Though at the rate he's losing fluid . . .

Lou hurriedly grabbed Bandit's big buffalo robe and heaved open the trapdoor again.

"Come on, Mutt," she said, and the dog ran over to her. "Down."

At her command, Mutt leaped down into the tunnel. Lou was about to follow on the ladder when her eye rested on her carpetbag.

The laudanum! She recalled with a grimace a particularly unwelcome side effect of opium—constipation, sometimes so severe that several very uncomfortable days could pass before anything came out. Perhaps if I can spoon a little of it into his mouth, she thought, it'll stop the cramps and he can get some decent sleep.

"Stay, Mutt!" she shouted down into the tunnel. "I'll be right there." The dog wagged his tail and sat.

She rummaged around in her bag and located the bottle. There was still perhaps a spoonful left in it, even after the enormous dose she had administered to the two prospectors. She brought it over to the bed and poured a few drops into a spoon—Bandit had none of her tolerance for the drug, and so she would have to be very careful not to give him too much. She inserted the spoon gently between Bandit's parched, cracked lips. He coughed, but seemed to keep the medicine down.

Good, she thought. Now let's go get something for the fever. She climbed down the ladder again, where Mutt was dutifully waiting for her. She and Mutt hurried along the tunnel and to the cave, where to her relief she found the first rays of daylight just peeking over the ridge.

"Stay here a minute," she said to Mutt, and quickly retraced her steps. In the cabin, Bandit was still unconscious and breathing raggedly—but regularly. She made sure he was tucked in under a pile of blankets, took down his rifle from above the door, slung her pack over her back, and removed from her carpetbag the key to her father's palace car. Throwing her snowshoes and a shovel through the trapdoor opening, she slid down the ladder like a raindrop.

Back at the cave, Lou lashed on her snowshoes and threw the buffalo robe over her shoulders. I'm strong enough to bear its weight now, she thought.

Mutt watched her quizzically, unused to going out without Bandit.

"We're going back to where you found me, Mutt," she told him. "There's medicine there, and your papa needs some. Let's go."

She kept the rifle in one hand, at the ready, and used the long-handled shovel as a walking stick. With faithful, formidable Mutt by her side, she began the long hike over the ridge and downhill to the railroad tracks.

—∞—

LOU HAD HIKED FOR the better part of two hours—she'd never be as fast on snowshoes as Bandit—when the abandoned train at last came into view, sitting desolate and snowblown on its frozen iron wheels. For a brief moment, she almost didn't recognize the thing that had once been such an important part of her life, this last train to Frisco. Now it all seemed like a strange dream—weirder even than the ones the laudanum had given her—instead of something from her very recent past. So much had changed since then, both around her and within her.

The palace car had tall, concave wind drifts swept high against its sides, but fortunately the wide baggage car had protected its forward door from the worst of it. Nonetheless, it took a good hour to shovel away the crusted snow and painstakingly chip the ice from the doorframe. She steeled herself, put the key into the lock, and turned.

To her surprise, the lock mechanism worked easily, but even after having been freed from its carapace of snow and ice, the door remained frozen shut. She threw her body against it four or five times, but then had to stop, sore and exhausted. Lou knew that every passing moment might cost Bandit his life, so she scanned her environment to see if another idea would come to her. A little distance from the tracks, she spied a winter-killed tree about four inches in diameter. She ran to it with hatchet in hand, cut it down quickly and trimmed away the branches to fashion a heavy pole of about eight feet in length. This she dragged, a few inches at a time, through the snow to the palace car. Ten feet from the door, gasping for breath, she let the heavy thing fall and readied herself.

Lou knelt, wrapped her arms around the log, and rolled it onto her thigh. Then, with every bit of her newfound strength, she stood, the log wavering around its midpoint like the arm of a scale. She very nearly dropped it, but before her grip could fail she mustered up her resolve and ran—as quickly as snowshoes would allow—at the palace car door, holding the log at her side like a battering ram. Luck was with her; she struck the door square on, and with a loud crack and slow creak it swung slowly inward. Lou dropped her lance and danced in the snow, and Mutt gamboled and barked around her.

No time to lose now, she thought. Lou went into the palace car that she had left behind only four months before, and though she remembered every detail of its layout, she couldn't recall a thing she had done in the car, other than dose herself with laudanum and sleep. It had taken Bandit and the High Sierra to rouse her, not only from her opium dream but from the sleepwalking life that she had lived, joylessly trying to be someone she was not, or—even worse—trying not to be who she was.

She located the medical kit and stuffed it into her rucksack. She hopped down from the car, pulled the door tight, and locked it again.

After lashing on her snowshoes and carefully checking the condition of the rifle—as Bandit had taught her—she and Mutt went back up the mountainside, step by painful step.

"How you and Bandit managed to drag me up this slope," she said to the dog, "I will never understand." He looked at her fondly and barked, as if to say that it had been worth whatever effort he'd put into it.

Halfway to the ridge overlooking their valley and the little cabin, Lou had to stop and rest. Her stomach was growling, so for a few minutes she looked around to see if there might be any berries that had gone uneaten this deep into winter. Finding nothing, she was about to hoist her pack again when she spied something in the snow that sent a chill down her spine: bear tracks, and fresh ones at that. Someone else had been looking for berries here too, and not very long ago.

"Mutt, look." She pointed at the tracks, and Mutt sniffed them carefully, hackles rising. "Keep an eye out," she said. "We're almost home."

Mutt kept close to her, and three-quarters of an hour later, over the ridge and in the deep shelter of their valley once again, the cave entrance came into view. She was about to hurry inside and to the tunnel when Mutt darted in front of her, crouched, and began to growl in a most unsettling way.

"What's wrong, Mutt?" she asked him. She was answered by a deep, guttural grunt, and from the depths of the cave came a very lean black bear, slavering and looking hungrily at Mutt and Lou. Mutt stood his ground, barking and snarling at the approaching bear.

Slowly Lou unslung her rifle from her shoulder, worked the action, and leveled the gun at the bear as calmly as she had seen Bandit do a dozen times before. "Shoo!" she yelled, waving her free arm. "Go on! Get out of my cave! Move, or I swear I'll shoot! I don't want to hurt you, but I *will*!"

The bear snorted and half reared on its haunches, but it seemed to sense in Lou a resolve that after such a long sleep it was unable to match. With surprising speed, the animal bolted past Mutt and Lou, and the two of them trotted into the tunnel and ran its length back to the cabin.

"*Please* let him be all right, Lord," she said out loud at the bottom of the ladder, and then, as her foot was on the first rung, she stopped. *No*, she thought, *he wouldn't want it this way.* "Lord," she resumed, bowing her head, "what I really want to say is . . . *thank you.* Thank you for giving me life, and for letting me feel your presence. And thank you for bringing such a truly wonderful man into it. For however long we may have. That's all."

Mutt looked up at her and barked.

"And for a very wonderful dog," she added, which set his tail wagging.

⁓

BANDIT WAS STILL UNCONSCIOUS when she returned to the cabin. Lou sat down on the edge of the bed and felt his forehead. While it was still on fire, he had not soiled the bed. The laudanum had worked!

"I'm back, dearest," she whispered. "I brought you some medicine."

Lou opened the medical kit and found a little booklet of instructions. Her father had taken care to equip her palace car with the latest medications, and as she scanned the list, one caught her eye—a very new drug out of Germany called aspirin.

"Aspirin promises to be the wonder drug of 1899," the pamphlet read. "It drives away the worst head and body aches and, even more important, reduces or eliminates fever."

She rummaged through the kit's many little bottles and containers until she found a glass vial full of white tablets and labeled

BAYER & COMPANY. ASPIRIN.
Recommended dose for body aches and fevers, two to four tablets.

Four tablets it is, she thought, shaking them out into her palm. She put her free hand under the back of Bandit's head and raised it a little.

"Honey," she said, "I need you to take this." With that she eased the pills one by one into his mouth, and tipped a glass of water against his lips. Bandit coughed, and Lou feared he'd spit out the aspirin, but instead he choked down the water and the pills in a kind of convulsive swallow.

"That's right, my love," she said softly, her words a prayer. "Stay with me now. Your Lou is with you always."

Lou put her head down on Bandit's chest and listened to his strong heart thudding inside. She stayed there quietly for a few minutes, until she was surprised to feel his hand weakly clench her arm. She sat up, studied his face, and saw that a tear had oozed out of the corner of his eye.

It's probably the fever, she thought, wiping it away.

IT TOOK TWO FRAUGHT days, but the new wonder drug aspirin did, in fact, work wonders on Bandit's fever. He felt progressively cooler as time went on, and the laudanum kept his bowels in check, although Lou was careful always to give him very little—and progressively less with each dose. She didn't want any repeat of the problems she had had. Soon he was able to sit up in bed, talk with his usual energy, and keep water down. Then it was broth and finally beans.

Despite his improvement, he remained bedridden and debilitated for more than a week, without venturing any farther than the chamber pot. Lou tended to him day and night, taking pleasure in giving him sips of water and tiny bites of food, and spending much of the day—other than feeding and letting Mutt go out—snuggling against him in their bed.

The following week, Bandit insisted on being up and about again, try as she might to get him to take it easy. He could not be prevented from restocking the depleted woodbin, refilling the water barrel with fresh snow, and even—on the first Saturday he could manage it—preparing a bath for the two of them under the tall and fragrant ponderosas. Lou couldn't measure her happiness at his recovery, and he looked at her admiringly—lovingly, even—when she told him how she had snowshoed down to the palace car and back again, alone, doing what she could to save his life.

There were bear tracks around the cabin almost every morning now, as the scrawny animals began foraging for scraps and garbage. And each afternoon, the creek swelled and throbbed with meltwater. Spring was coming, and barring another untimely blizzard—always a possibility in these treacherous mountains—in another few weeks she would be able to return to her train and wait there for the track-clearing crews to reach the abandoned Frisco Express.

That would mean saying goodbye to Bandit, and Mutt, and Deborah, and to their cozy bed in their tidy cabin. Yet Lou had begun to make peace with the notion that perhaps it must be that way; that Bandit had come here for solitude, and with an open heart had shared his winter with her. Now, she knew, she might well have to leave him be again. Even though she loved him utterly, she knew now that loving *him* could not be enough reason for her to stay. If he loved *her*, too, that might be different, but Bandit was a man who'd known love once and had seen it leave.

Perhaps, she thought, he could still find a space in his heart for love to grow again. Yet Lou was no longer a coddled city girl. She had become a woman, and could now understand that even the strongest woman can do only so much for her man; some things a man has to do for himself. Unless and until he could give himself to her fully and without reservation, she could never be his. Only then could the past be the past forever. She had believed otherwise, even very recently, but Lou was wise enough these days to understand what she had been up against the whole time.

She knew that she could never compete with a memory, so long as that memory still held sway over his heart. And she loved herself too much to allow herself to do so.

24

❧

The Rescue Mission

Sierra Pacific Railroad Headquarters
New York City

"Bartholomew," Judge MacGregor said to the president of the Sierra Pacific, "I am officially out of patience. In truth, I have been out of patience for months, but for quite some time you had a good excuse, at least. Now, though, the reports are of an early spring in the Sierras, and still I sit here, waiting for you to give the word for an attempt to reach my stranded daughter!"

The railroad man held out his hands. "Your Honor, just this morning I received some encouraging news. Our depot in Reno tells me that they have just taken delivery of the huge rotary snowplow locomotive that Senator Depew and Governor Roosevelt steered in our direction. This machine can clear tracks like no previous machine could. It's still slow, but inch by inch it will eat up whatever's between the Nevada border and your private car."

"Then have you sent it out?"

"I gave them the instruction to depart Reno immediately, of course. It's started on its slow journey."

"How may I get aboard?"

"Our passenger trains run considerably faster than the snowplow," Bartholomew said. "How soon can you leave for Reno?"

"In an hour, if necessary!"

"Good. Of course, we will defray the cost of an express car to meet the snowplow. You'll certainly be aboard by the time it enters the High Sierra, and you'll be the first on the scene."

"Thank you, Bartholomew," Judge MacGregor said, his voice catching. "At the very least . . . I want to be the person who finds my daughter's remains. Her mother and I would both want it that way."

"I don't need to remind you, Your Honor, but I wouldn't give up hope quite yet. As I said the first time we met, if your daughter has a guardian angel who has been looking over her—and I believe everyone does—she may well still be alive."

"That is my fondest hope," the judge replied. "Though I have had to temper my expectations against the enormity of the challenge she has faced since November. Who knows what torments she has been suffering all this time, if God has even been merciful enough to allow her to live."

25

The Thaw

Late March

They were awakened by the crash of icicles falling from the eaves.

"It's warming up fast," Bandit said.

"Um hmm," Lou said drowsily.

"Spring is beautiful up here. I wish you could see it."

"I can only imagine. I think winter's magnificent."

They lay there for a few more minutes, until Lou stirred again.

"Scooch out, you big lump, and I'll get the fire going and make us some coffee."

"Not yet," he said. "Let's lie here a little while longer."

"You won't have to ask me twice." She snuggled up against him, reveling in the feel of his skin.

"Lou?"

"That's my name."

"I've been doing a lot of thinking."

"What else is new? That's what you *do*, Bandit. You *think*."

"I know, but this time I've been thinking about . . . *us*."

"Us?"

"Yes, us. You and me."

"Now this *is* new," she said. "What have you been thinking?"

"That I don't want you to leave. Lou, I want you to stay with me. Forever."

She lifted her head. "Where did *that* come from?"

"My heart."

"I didn't mean it *literally*."

"Well, that's where it came from."

"But you like your solitude. And I've been keeping you from it for more than four months now."

"Then let me put it another way. Do you want to go back to your old life?"

"Not really, no."

"Why not?"

"Because I can never explain what has happened to me this winter. Not the rescue, or the snow, or even those horrible men who barged in here. And my father and everyone will want their Louisa back. But she's become someone else now. She's *Lou*."

He leaned up on one elbow, dumping her off his shoulder.

"That's pretty much the way I feel, too. And I *do* like my solitude— or did, until you came along. But now I feel that, without you, solitude would be more like loneliness."

She lay quietly for a while, watching him study her face. "We might have talked about this a *long* time ago, you know," she said. "Now the whole world is thawing out, and before we know it my father will be here with a rescue party. You must recognize that I can't very well tell him to turn around and go back home."

"I know . . . believe me, I know," he said. "And I know I *should* have brought all this up long ago. But I didn't want you to feel obligated to stay and not return to your real life."

"Bandit," she said with a trace of pique, "*this* is my real life now. Surely you have known that for some time."

He bit his lower lip. "I suppose I have."

"Then come out and tell me the plain truth," she said. "You've never lied to me before, and I don't want you to start now. Why did you wait until *now* to ask me to stay here?"

"Because . . . when my wife—Emma—was dying, I made her a promise."

"And there it is," Lou said, looking away. "I should have known. God, I really am stupid sometimes." She closed her eyes. "Go on, tell me."

"First of all, you're not stupid," Bandit said.

"Don't try to butter me up, lump. What was the promise?"

"I promised her on her deathbed that I would never marry again."

A tear squeezed out of the side of Lou's eye. "Of course you did." She opened her eyes and looked at him. "May I ask whether she requested this promise, or you offered it?"

"I offered it."

"And may I ask how she received it?"

"She was angry. She told me not to be a damn fool."

"Good girl," Lou said softly.

"She told me that no matter how much I loved her, and that she loved me, there was a reason that the marriage vows include 'until death do us part.' She said that I had already fulfilled the only vow she had ever asked me to take."

"You know, I think I would really like Emma," Lou said. "Even if she were still your wife."

"I think you would, too. Now Lou, you know that I take a degree of pride in being a man of my word."

"A *degree*? That's an understatement."

He ignored her. "So even after you'd been here for a while, and things, you know—my thoughts about you—*changed* . . . I told myself that, like it or not, I'd given my word, and I would keep it."

"Can you just skip ahead and tell me whether I'm going back to New York or not?"

"That's entirely up to you," Bandit said. "But as I said, I want you to stay."

"And I'd like to stay. But Bandit, I can't—I won't—stay on as your friend, or hunting companion, or whatever it is that I have been. It's time for me to start my life again, and as much as I'd like to have you in it . . . I need far more than we have now. I want to be able to give myself fully, body and soul, to someone."

"I know that, Lou, and I—"

"Let me finish while I still have the courage to," she said. "I felt love for Henry, but I know now that it was more an affectionate kind of love than it was *true love*. True love fills to overflowing the mind, the spirit, and the body, until there's simply no room left for anything else. I didn't know what *that* felt like until I came here."

"And do you now?"

She looked steadily at him. "Oh yes. Without a shadow of a doubt. Because it's what I feel when I see you, or hear your voice, or think about you, or feel your skin against mine. I love you more than I ever thought it possible to love anything or anyone. And I love myself now, too, because I've found my *true* self at last . . . and in large part because you found me first."

"You can't begin to know how happy that makes me, Lou," he said. "For so long I've tried to tell myself that what I have been feeling for you wasn't *love*. It was tenderness, or protection, or all of that mixed up together. But it *was* love, true love, all along. From the first moment you pointed that derringer at me."

"Without cocking the hammer," she said wryly.

His blue eyes sparkled at her. "Now, Lou—may I ask you a question, dear?"

"You know you can ask me anything, you big ogre."

"Will you marry me?"

She sat bolt upright in bed. "Did I hear you correctly?"

"I believe you did, yes. I am asking you to be my wife, Lou. Of course, if you need time to consider—"

"I do."

He nodded. "I understand. You are welcome to take all the time you need. The offer's good for the rest of my life."

"I didn't mean 'I do' as in 'yes, I'd like more time to consider.' I meant 'yes, *I do*' as in 'yes, I want to marry you!' There's nothing I'd like more." She paused. "But I do have to ask . . . what about your vow to never marry again?"

"*Someone* I know," he said, "asked me once whether I might not really *want* to forgive myself for my wife's death."

"And was this *someone* onto something?"

"She was indeed. You see, this person helped me to understand that the vow I made at Emma's death wasn't to Emma at all. It was to *myself*, because I had known joy, and then it was gone—and that *hurt*. So I promised myself I would never feel that kind of pain again. What I didn't realize is that the only way never to feel that kind of pain . . . is never to feel joy. Because joy doesn't stay forever; that's not its nature. But now I've learned—I *know*—that whether it lasts for a lifetime or only for a season, joy is *always* worth the risk. It was you who taught me that."

She rested her hand on his cheek. "We've taught each other the most important lessons of all, haven't we?"

He nodded, tears in his eyes. She leaned over and kissed him on the lips, for the very first time. He kissed her back, passionately.

"So do I have your answer?" he asked.

"Most of it," she said, kissing him again. "The mind and soul part."

"What else is there?"

"The *body* part, silly. Do you remember how I told you I wanted to be Number Three-Oh-One?"

"How could I forget?" he said, rolling his eyes.

"Well, I've decided that's not good enough for me, either. Since we're both making a fresh start, I want a new count entirely."

"And so do I. Hello, Number One."

AFTER THEY HAD MADE love, they sat up in bed, sipping their morning coffee, which had never tasted quite so delicious.

"It seems that *at last* I've been officially ravished by a mountain man, after all," Lou said. "Even though it nearly took every trick in the book to make it happen."

He grinned. "Then perhaps we ought better to say that I've been ravished by a mountain lady."

"Either way, that was delightful. On every level. I haven't known what I've been missing."

"Nor have I, Lou. Nor have I."

They kissed—urgently and with intent now—and set their coffee mugs aside.

"I could get used to that," Lou mumbled later, after they had napped.

"I think you'd better."

"There is one little fly in the ointment," she said. "Just to prepare you. You'll recall I told you about the problems that scuttled my first engagement. Social problems."

"Yes, his family didn't see yours as high enough on the register to qualify for a marital union. Even though your father is a judge."

"Right. And while my family doesn't number among New York's Four Hundred, appearances *do* matter to them."

"And you're suggesting that marrying a mountain man may raise certain objections."

She bit her lower lip. "I can't lie to you. It will. Personally, I don't care, but we have to be prepared for me to be excommunicated. Which, by the way, won't change my mind one little bit, but still."

"They'd do that?"

"They may have to, if they wish to maintain their place in society. And you know how that is in New York."

"I do, dear. But try not to worry. I'm sure they won't object once they meet me."

Lou kissed his cheek. "I swear, no one could have more self-confidence than you do, Bandit."

"You must know by now that my *real* name isn't Bandit."

"Considering that I named you that, yes, I did know that much. And I know it's not that phony Robin Littlejohn handle you tried to fob off on me. But I've never pressed you about your real name. I reckoned you'd tell me if you wanted to."

"*Reckoned*? You're sounding like a *gen-u-ine* mountain lady these days!"

"You're rubbing off on me, I guess. But in truth, since we are to marry, I suppose I ought to know your legal name. I will want to take it for my own."

"What if you don't like it?"

"Don't like it? What kind of name would I not like? I've been calling you Bandit for months, and I've liked that well enough."

"Good point. Well then, my name is William."

"William is a very dignified name," Lou said with an approving nod. "Yes, I like it. Do you prefer William or Bill?"

"When I was a boy my family called me Billy, but that was some time ago. It's been William for quite a while now."

"Very well, William it shall be."

"I wish you'd still call me Bandit, actually. I feel more at home with that name."

"That's a relief, because I like it better, too," Lou said. "Now your surname, if you please, so that I may complete the picture of my future husband. And see how *Lou* sounds with my new last name."

"Naturally. It's Van Cantlandt. I'm William Van Cantlandt of New York City."

Her jaw dropped. *"Excuse me?"*

"Excuse you what?"

"Did you say *Van Cantlandt*? Did I hear that correctly?"

He nodded gravely. "You did."

"You can't mean . . ."

"I'm afraid so. *The* Van Cantlandts of Park Avenue."

Lou smacked her forehead with her palm. "The Van Cantlandts are members of the Four Hundred, you know."

"Oh, believe me, I know."

She closed her jaw with some effort. "Your family is said to have a hundred million."

"Since you and I have no secrets left, it's closer to a hundred-fifty, but who's counting? I made fifty of that myself when I was on Wall Street."

"Good night," Lou said. "Now I understand why you were so confident my father wouldn't object to our union."

"There *are* advantages to being a Van Cantlandt, though until just now I really didn't want to avail myself of any of them again."

"Why didn't you tell me before this?" Lou asked.

He sighed. "I learned very early in life to be careful about my name. People make all sorts of judgments, good or bad, the second they hear it. When I came out here, I was thoroughly sick and tired of all that. I wanted to be Robin Littlejohn so that I could be *myself* for the first time in my life, whoever that was. And frankly, when you named me Bandit, I liked it even better since Wall Street types like me are nothing if not a bunch of bandits."

She kissed him. "You're not a *real* bandit . . . even though you *have* completely stolen my heart."

"Drat it all, Lou, I wish I'd thought of that," he said.

"And I wish I'd thought of 'when love shows up at your door, you have to let it in.'"

"Even if it's only a cabin door?"

"Especially then."

"So my current abode aside, do you think your father will find my suit to marry you an acceptable one?"

Lou laughed. "I should say so. To get into the Four Hundred, he'd probably marry you himself."

"You do have a nice laugh, Mrs. Van Cantlandt," he said.

26

A Change of Clothing

She left her leather trousers, denim shirt, and old belt folded neatly on their bed. "Another reason to come back," she told him.

Otherwise, she had packed her carpetbag and put on the lovely velvet traveling suit that she had last worn in November while lying on a travois, bumping up the mountain to Bandit's cabin.

"Well, this feels odd," Lou said, looking down at herself. She looked again very much like Louisa MacGregor, if more lean and taut, and her skin bronzed from the clear winter sun.

"I barely recognize you," Bandit said.

"That's probably because I'm fully clothed."

"No doubt. I'm going to miss that."

"Unless you change your mind about marrying me, you'll be able to see it as much as you like."

"I will never change my mind about that," Bandit said. "Say . . . we'll probably have a while in the palace car before the Sierra Pacific plow arrives. Are you sure you don't want to take your mountain clothes with you?"

"I might as well get used to these duds again. Will you be wearing your suit?"

"Don't you think that might be a little dishonest?"

"Dress for your audience, my dear. My father will drop over dead if he meets you in *that* getup."

"As if you won't look a sight in that dress and your snowshoes."

She laughed. "I probably have forgotten how to walk in anything but."

"Before we say goodbye to our cabin, at least for a while . . . there is one last thing."

He pulled the Oriental rug aside, opened the trapdoor, and vanished down the ladder. He was back in a couple minutes, carrying a leather Gladstone bag.

"Is that the bag you were raving about in your delirium?" she asked.

"I wasn't delirious when I told you about it, but yes, it is the same bag. Did you happen to look inside it?"

She shook her head. "Not in a million years. I'm not peeking inside anything of yours again, unless you are around, and it would have been especially bad luck to look when you were hovering between life and death."

"Then let's have a look together," he said, setting the bag on the floor between them. He knelt and undid the straps that held the top closed.

She looked over his shoulder as he took from the Gladstone bag a heavy canvas sack, tied at the top with a leather thong. He opened the bag. It was three-quarters full of twenty-dollar gold pieces.

"My word!" she said. "For a fact, you weren't lying when you said you had valuables stashed down there."

"Three years is a long time without *any* luxuries at all," he said. "Every year, I ordered a sack of coffee from Delmonico's, ham, beans, and so on. I had to pay for them somehow, and what's better than gold?"

"You are one of a kind, Bandit Van Cantlandt."

"But *this* is the most valuable thing of all," he said, pulling out an envelope with his neat cursive writing on the outside, which read:

TO MY EXECUTOR

"Your executor?"

"After I drank that contaminated water, I figured that I faced long odds of making it," he said. "And if it hadn't been for you, I wouldn't have. So before I got sick, I wrote something down for you. Would you care to read it?"

"It's addressed to your executor, not to me."

"And he would have read it to you. Since I'm alive and have no need for him to do the honors, you may go right ahead."

She took a single sheet of folded paper out of the envelope and smoothed it out. It had been written with their pine cone ink. She read:

To Mr. R. Johnston, Esq.,
Executor for the Estate of William T. Van Cantlandt.

"What's the *T* stand for?" she asked.

"Thayer. It's my mother's maiden name."

"Ah," she said, and resumed reading.

My dear Mr. Johnston:

> *I regret that this may be something of a bolt from*
> *the blue, but I come now before you being of sound*

mind and understanding, if currently somewhat enfeebled in body—the result of consuming water contaminated by a putrefying animal.

When I settled my affairs before I came west, I had been recently widowed, and so naturally I bequeathed the corpus of my estate to my parents. Recently, however, much has changed in my life. I have met, and will marry, a truly wonderful woman, Miss Louisa MacGregor. Her father is a prominent New York judge, who is most likely already among your acquaintance. Only the remoteness of our location, and our resulting inability to travel, have prevented us from sanctifying our marital bond. Yet I assure you that we are fully married in spirit and only the formalities of legal marriage remain.

As my parents, as well as my brother and sister, possess more than ample financial resources to last them through their natural lifetimes, I wish to cancel and withdraw my previous instructions, and bequeath my entire estate, net of any funeral and burial expenses, to my fiancée Miss MacGregor. This includes my portfolio of stocks, bonds, and other instruments, and all of my personal effects, whether located in New York City or elsewhere in any part of the world. This would also include my apartments in London and Paris, as well as my town house on Park Avenue.

I would invite my parents, brother, and sister to select such mementos from my effects as would bring my memory kindly to mind. One telegram a year from their son and brother has not been enough to reward their steadfast love. Please assure them that it has always been returned, and that my withdrawal into the remote parts of our country neither is, nor has ever been, any reflection upon them, but rather one of my own desire to find personal peace after a period of great turmoil.

I have found that peace now, and more, as evidenced by my engagement to Miss MacGregor. In life or in death, I will love her with all my heart.

I have sealed this bond with my thumbprint in my own blood. It is comparable to those I have left on other documents in your custody.

Yours very sincerely,

William T. Van Cantlandt

Donner Pass, California
March 1900.

Lou set the paper down gently and hugged Bandit, kissing him softly on the lips. "You wrote this *before* you asked me to marry you," she whispered. "Yet in it you call me your fiancée."

"I was planning to ask you to marry me before I fell ill," he said. "But then doing so while being hoisted on and off the thunder mug didn't seem very romantic."

"Maybe not . . . but I would have said yes just the same."

WHEN NOTHING REMAINED BUT to depart, Lou took a last look around their tidy cabin. "It feels so odd to be leaving here," she said. "So much has happened in this little home of ours."

"You saved my bacon a few times," he said.

"And you mine. I'd be tempted to call it even . . . but then you ravished me. Half a dozen times thus far, in fact." She laughed. "But who's counting?"

"We are," he said. "So be careful, because I might well ravish you again in your palace car."

"I'll be disappointed if you don't."

"Once again, we see eye to eye. Now let's get on our way. Mutt!"

"Wait! What about Deborah?"

Bandit opened his rucksack, and Deborah poked her little grey head out.

"There's our girl," Lou said.

"We're a family of four now," he said with a smile.

WHEN THEY ARRIVED AT the railroad tracks, they found that the snow had melted almost entirely away from the palace car door. Lou unlocked it, and it swung open smoothly.

"There's a rather severe dent in this door," Bandit observed. "Wonder how that got here?"

"I'll tell you the story later, over some ham," Lou said. "My father will have it repaired, I'm sure."

Bandit climbed up into the palace car and had a quick look around to make sure no wildlife had taken up residence. He scrounged up a bucket and then went out again to collect some fuel from a large pile of coal that was peeking above the shrinking snowdrifts.

Soon the iron stove was roaring and the palace car was almost as cozy and warm as their little cabin in the high, hidden valley. They sat together on the velvet settee, looking a bit incongruous—Louisa in her lovely traveling habit, and Bandit in his leather leggings and shirt.

A quick search of the baggage car didn't produce any more meat, but they did find a burlap sack of potatoes—sprouting eyes in every direction—and a real luxury, a small bag of unspoiled coffee.

"It'll be just like Delmonico's tonight," Bandit said.

"Just like back home in our cabin."

"Say, Lou. Speaking of *home*. What would you like to do about our wedding? I assume you'd want it in New York?"

"Would you?"

"It's been quite a while since I've seen my family, so I'd very much hope so."

"I'm in agreement. The bigger question is . . . what after that?"

"You mean Park Avenue or Donner Pass?"

"Everything, I suppose," she said. "Will you want to resume your Wall Street life?"

"I think that ship has sailed," Bandit said. "I think I'd much prefer to spend every moment with you. What would you think about living in London or Paris for a while? As you may have noticed in my letter, I own properties there."

"I seem to recall telling you once that as a girl I dreamed of having an apartment in Paris. So . . . I'd love to!"

"Then it's agreed. In spring we will sail for France. Or wherever else you might like."

"On one condition," Lou said. "That we come back to our cabin for the autumn."

"So long as it's not aboard the last train to Frisco," he said with a wink.

27

Reunion

Ten days later

They heard it—a deep rumble reverberating along the steel tracks, through the wheels of the palace car, and into their bones—long before it came into view. Lou ran to the door of the carriage, pulled it open, and leaned out. Coming slowly up the grade from the east was a gigantic locomotive, angrily belching black smoke and pushing an enormous whirling blade, which was throwing snow right and left.

"It's the clearing train!" she called back to Bandit, who was sitting on the settee in his business suit, complete with his ruby studs and cuff links. He was clean-shaven and smelled faintly of sandalwood, looking every bit the Wall Street swell he once had been.

"Good news!" he said with a broad smile. "Now go on out there and meet the train. I'd bet everything I have that your father is aboard."

She smiled back at him, threw her coat over her shoulders, and ran out into the cold. When the plow locomotive squealed hissing to a stop behind the palace car, she trotted along the tracks toward it. From the front of the train—from the engineer's cab itself—her father jumped down, going up to his ankles in the melting snow. He ran toward his daughter, laughing and crying all at once.

"Oh, my sweet, darling Louisa!" he said as they embraced.

"My dear father," she said, kissing his cheek. "I've missed you and mother so terribly!"

He held her out at arm's length. "It really *is* you," he said, his eyes welling. "I'm ashamed to say that I'd almost given up hope."

"If there's anything this trial has taught me," she said, smiling back at him, "it's that hope is lost only when we let it go."

"Such wisdom!" Judge MacGregor exclaimed. "Why, my dear, you ought to be the judge!"

"I hardly think so," she said. "But I did have a wonderful teacher. I should like to introduce you to the man who both rescued me and preserved my life all these long months."

"And I should like to thank him," the judge said. "I owe him everything."

"He's waiting for us in your car," Lou said, taking her beaming father's hand.

"I simply cannot believe it," he said as they crunched toward the palace car. "The very instant we arrive in San Francisco, I am telephoning to your mother. Unlike your father, that woman never lost faith that we would be reunited. She said from the start that a guardian angel would watch over you."

"I cannot wait to hear her voice," Lou said. "And she was right. I *did* have a guardian angel looking over me. You're about to meet him!"

She threw open the palace car door and helped her father up the stairs. "Father," she said, gesturing grandly with her arm, "may I present to you—"

But there was no one in the palace car parlor. No Bandit—only the soft hiss of the coal stove.

"I don't understand," she mused. "Perhaps he was unwell and needed to lie down."

"Then we must look in the sleeping quarters," the judge said. "I brought Dr. Mansfield along with me, so if this generous fellow is ill, we shall do whatever is required to restore him to health!"

Lou hastened to the door of their sleeping quarters and threw it open. There was no sign of Bandit there, either. But there *was* a men's suit laid out on their bed, and freshly polished shoes sitting on the floor in front of it.

"What in the devil?" Judge MacGregor said under his breath. "Did the man simply vanish?"

Lou looked around, and even oddly thought to look under the bed, where Bandit had found her hiding so many months before. But even *he* wouldn't pull such a stunt, she thought.

"I confess I don't understand at all—"

"Hello?" came a familiar voice from the parlor. "Is anyone in here?"

Lou and her father darted out of the sleeping compartment to find Bandit standing in the parlor, dressed in his mountain-man clothes. He removed his beaten-up old hat and bowed deeply in the direction of the judge.

"Judge MacGregor, I presume," he said. "It is a pleasure to meet you, Your Honor."

The judge looked at Bandit, then at his daughter, and then back at Bandit again.

"*This* is the man who rescued you?" he asked Lou.

"It is, Father. And more than rescued me. Truly he is the man who helped me to become a woman."

The judge scowled at her, and his face darkened. "What in thunder does that mean, *become a woman*?" He turned to Bandit, looking him up and down. "Sir, I'll thank you to give me a full and frank explanation of my daughter's statement. For more than four months, she has been under your influence—your spell, perhaps. And now she states that you have made her into a *woman*? Tell me candidly, sir, for I am not a man to whom people lie with impunity! So do not, if you have an honorable bone in your body, trifle with me now. *Have you ravished my daughter?*"

Bandit looked over at Lou. "I see where you get it now," he said with a grin.

Lou shook her head at him. "Not a good time."

"Answer my question, sir!"

"Your Honor, I fully understand and respect your concern. Please be assured that I have taken no advantage of your daughter. My sole interest has been to preserve her for your reunion, though most of the credit for that goes to Lou herself. Your daughter has become quite the mountain lady."

"*Lou*? What manner of—"

"It's just what he calls me, Father. He never would call me Louisa, except once or twice . . . and that was only when he had a high fever."

"Sir," Bandit said, "I believe that what your Louisa meant is that she has become not only an accomplished outdoorswoman, but also has revealed herself to me as the woman I wish, more than anything, to spend my life with. I therefore ask you, sir, and with respect, for your consent to our nuptials."

"Nuptials!" the judge bellowed. "*Nuptials*? A matrimonial union between my darling, only daughter, finely brought up in the very best of society . . . and a . . . a . . . *mountain man*?" He spluttered to a stop, out of words.

"In effect, yes sir."

"Preposterous," the judge said. "I regret that I must object in the most strenuous terms."

"But Father—"

"Louisa, my dear, if you would—please allow this . . . fellow and me a few moments in private."

"I will do nothing of the sort," Lou said. Her eyes sparkled up at Bandit. "I want this *fellow* to be my husband, Father. I love him with every fiber of my being. He has made, and makes, me happy in a way I never thought possible. And throughout my stay with him, he has been a complete gentleman. There has been no ravishment." She turned her head away from her father and winked at Bandit.

"I am at a loss for words," Judge MacGregor said. "Truly at a loss." He paused, studying his shoes and swaying back and forth on his toes, and at last he looked up again at Bandit. "While happiness is the thing I've always wanted most for my beloved daughter, until this moment I have never seen it shine so brightly from her eyes."

Lou tugged on her father's arm. "That is because my heart is full to bursting, Father. With love and gratitude to this man—to you and Mother—and to God."

The judge pursed his lips for a long moment. "In the face of such opposition, duty compels me to overrule my own objection," he said with a sudden smile. "Therefore, sir, if you are indeed the man who has wrought this change in my Louisa . . . then yes, I will gladly consent to your marriage. Without reservation and with a full heart."

Lou threw herself into Bandit's arms and covered his face with kisses.

"I thank you most sincerely, sir," Bandit said, when Lou let him go and again stood by his side. "And we would consider it a special honor if you would officiate at our wedding, once we return to New York— and your entire family, as well as my own, are able to celebrate with us."

"Naturally," the judge said. "Do I take it, then, that your family resides in New York?"

"They do, though I've been out here for three years now. But it's long past time for me to go back, for a little while at least. And for Lou, too, of course."

"Capital! Then it shall be exactly as you say. Yet it strikes me as somewhat odd that I don't yet even know the name of this man who has so transformed my precious Louisa, and who will soon join our family! May I inquire as to your identity?"

"Of course you may, Your Honor." Bandit stuck out his hand. "I am William Thayer Van Cantlandt, late of Park Avenue. More recently of Donner Pass."

The judge blanched. "You're *who*?"

"William Thayer Van Cantlandt, sir, at your service." He smiled at the judge's stunned expression. "But if you please . . . call me Bandit."

THE END

SINCE GRATITUDE IS ONE OF THE MAJOR THEMES OF THIS BOOK, I have been especially eager to write this little section.

I usually conclude my acknowledgments with my wife, but this time I will begin with her, because if I have a 'muse,' it must be she. I am blessed and grateful for her constant support, encouragement, and wise counsel.

I am also thankful to my publisher, Ashwood Press, for in essence (and with their usual good cheer) daring me to write a romance novel. As with so many other things, this experience taught me to remain open to possibility.

And as always, my humble thanks go out to my many enthusiastic readers everywhere. Without you, I could not exist at all.

Robert Brighton

About the Author

ROBERT BRIGHTON IS AN AUTHORITY ON THE GILDED Age, an inveterate explorer, and the author of the Avenging Angel Detective Agency™ Mysteries and other titles.

He began writing fiction after spending four years researching the liminal period of 1898–1905, in which his novels are set. Prior to that, he has been a bison rancher, mule handler, vintage automobile restorer, and has made several other equally quixotic career choices.

When he's not writing, he's either spending time with his wife and their two cats or exploring some new part of the world. He has an enthusiasm for Japanese tin toys, antique weather instruments, and anything mechanical.

Winter in the High Sierra is his first romance novel but, with any luck, not his last.

Find out more at
RobertBrightonAuthor.com

www.ingramcontent.com/pod-product-compliance
Lightning Source LLC
Chambersburg PA
CBHW020655010826
48969CB00013B/2020